RAVEN

GEMS OF WOLFE ISLAND TWO

HELEN HARDT

RAVEN

GEMS OF WOLFE ISLAND TWO

WOLFES OF MANHATTAN EIGHT

Helen Hardt

HARDT & SONS ♥

HARDT & SONS

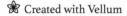 Created with Vellum

Happy New Year! May 2022 bring you love, joy, peace, and prosperity.

ALSO BY HELEN HARDT

Misadventures of a Good Wife (with Meredith Wild)

Misadventures with a Rockstar

The Cougar Chronicles:

The Cowboy and the Cougar

Calendar Boy

Daughters of the Prairie:

The Outlaw's Angel

Lessons of the Heart

Song of the Raven

Collections:

Destination Desire

Her Two Lovers

Non-Fiction:

got style?

PRAISE FOR HELEN HARDT

WOLFES OF MANHATTAN

"It's hot, it's intense, and the plot starts off thick and had me completely spellbound from page one."

~**The Sassy Nerd Blog**

"Helen Hardt...is a master at her craft."

~**K. Ogburn, Amazon**

"Move over Steel brothers... Rock is *everything!*"

~**Barbara Conklin-Jaros, Amazon**

"Helen has done it again. She winds you up and weaves a web of intrigue."

~**Vicki Smith, Amazon**

FOLLOW ME SERIES

"Hardt spins erotic gold..."

"Talon has hit my top five list...up there next to Jamie Fraser and Gideon Cross."

~*USA Today* **bestselling author Angel Payne**

"Talon and Jade's instant chemistry heats up the pages..."

~**RT Book Reviews**

"Sorry Christian and Gideon, there's a new heartthrob for you to contend with. Meet Talon. Talon Steel."

~**Booktopia**

"Such a beautiful torment—the waiting, the anticipation, the relief that only comes briefly before more questions arise, and the wait begins again... Check. Mate. Ms. Hardt..."

~**Bare Naked Words**

"Made my heart stop in my chest. Helen has given us such a heartbreakingly beautiful series."

~**Tina, Bookalicious Babes**

BLOOD BOND SAGA

"An enthralling and rousing vampire tale that will leave readers waiting for the sequel."

~**Kirkus Reviews**

"Dangerous and sexy. A new favorite!"

~*New York Times* **bestselling author Alyssa Day**

"A dark, intoxicating tale."

~**Library Journal**

"Helen dives into the paranormal world of vampires and makes it her own."

~Tina, **Bookalicious Babes**

"Throw out everything you know about vampires—except for that blood thirst we all love and lust after in these stunning heroes—and expect to be swept up in a sensual story that twists and turns in so many wonderfully jaw-dropping ways."

~**Angel Payne,** *USA Today* **bestselling author**

WARNING

The Gems of Wolfe Island series contains adult language and scenes, including flashbacks of physical and sexual abuse. Please take note.

PROLOGUE

LUKE

The bus station is eerily quiet at three in the morning. I didn't think anyone in Manhattan ever slept. I'm not looking forward to a cross-country bus ride, but I'll be able to keep much more under the radar than if I tried flying or renting a car.

I bought my ticket with cash, and now I wait.

Until—

Something nudges the small of my back.

"Where the hell do you think you're going?" a deep voice says.

"Who the hell are you?" I begin to look over my shoulder but—

Fuck. It's a gun. It nudges harder into my back.

"You really didn't think you could hide from us, did you?"

"I don't know what you're talking about," I say, willing my voice not to crack.

I can handle whoever this is. I've handled worse.

Of course... When I had to handle worse, I wasn't a fucking stool pigeon.

"I think you know where this ends," the voice says.

"We'll see where it ends." I scan the station.

I see one security guard. Just one. No police officers.

I'm not sure how I can get the security guard's attention. I'm not sure if I even want to. Whoever this is, if he's anything like I used to be, he's already taken care of the security guard.

"What the fuck do you want?" I say through gritted teeth.

"Not much," he says. "Just your big head on a fucking silver platter...*Lucifer Raven*."

1

LUKE

*L*ucifer Raven.

I know the name, have said it in my mind, but when someone else says it in reference to me, it catapults me back.

I must face the sins of my past if I'm going to be worthy of Katelyn.

"You'd better have good news for me." I take a deep drink of the bottle of bourbon I'm holding.

"We found her," Dred, my head of security says. "She's on a private island in the South Pacific."

"How the fuck did you let this happen?" I demand.

"I'm sorry. It's her brother, the SEAL. He's got connections with the Wolfe family."

"Not the Wolfes of Manhattan."

"They're the ones."

"Fuck. When can I get there?"

"Your reservations are made. You'll be traveling under your alias."

"You want to give me a reason I shouldn't fire the lot of you?" I shoot daggers at him with my eyes.

"We found her, Raven. And believe me, Buck Moreno kept her hidden well."

"Yeah? I'll deal with you idiots when I get back. Give me the information."

Nine hours later I'm on the island with the knife I pilfered from one of the guards. Seems even the Wolfes' hired guns can be bought. The guy'll be toast by tomorrow, but he'll be rich toast. I made sure of that.

I down a few shots of bourbon, follow Dred's instructions and make my way to Emily's room. I pick the lock quickly and quietly and enter.

I inhale.

The milky and slightly gingery scent of Ivory soap. Emily uses it to clean her paint brushes. An easel is set up with a canvas and a work in progress.

It's a simple ocean scene, the operative word being simple. Emily has never lived up to her potential. Some of her abstracts are genius, but this? Any simpleton can paint an ocean, for fuck's sake.

She's done her best work while living with me. Even she admits that. I ought to destroy this piece of shit.

But I won't.

I'll sit here, inhaling the fresh scent of Ivory, which overpowers her own citrus and coconut fragrance.

I love her. I fucking love Emily Moreno. I've given her everything. Why does she want to leave me?

Why do they always *want to leave me?*

I cock my head when I hear the lock on the door click.

Emily enters, and she's wearing—

For fuck's sake, she's wearing a man's shirt. Not only a man's shirt but a man's shirt that's bright royal blue with palm trees and pink flamingos splattered all over it. Then I feel it—the familiar slithering of rage curling up my spine.

She gasps when she spies me sitting on the bed. I turn back to the canvas depicting the ocean scene.

I don't look up. I've become adept at controlling my rage...most of the time. I can play the role of an icy bystander...most of the time.

"Not your best work, Emily."

She doesn't reply.

"Then again, I was always your muse."

Still no reply.

"You didn't truly think you could escape from me, did you?" *I rise then and turn toward her, narrowing my eyes, trying to still the anger pulsating along with my rapidly beating heart.* "Pack your things. We're going home. Now."

"No," *she says.*

No. She knows better than that. But this "no" ignites something more in me. Makes me want her all the more. Makes me more determined than ever to have her.

I shake my head. "Whose shirt is that?"

"No one's."

I do my best to remain calm. "You're not that good a liar, Emily."

"How did you get in here?"

I scoff. "Really? You think I'm a vampire or something? That I need an invitation? We both knew I'd find you."

"But security—"

After all our time together, she still doesn't know who I am, what I'm capable of. "I know my way around the best security in *the world. How do you think I've remained in business so long? Now pack up."*

"No." She whips her hands to her hips, a look of amusing determination crossing her fine features.

So this is how it will be. Fine. She can show her strength.

And I'll show mine.

"This isn't up for negotiation, Emily."

"I'm not going."

I don't want to strike her. Truly, I don't. I don't do it often. Only when I have to. Only when she makes me.

I raise my fist—

She moves quick as lightning, ducking, and then she runs out the door, giving me a peek of her bare ass as she goes. My God, is she wearing nothing but another man's shirt?

I curl my fingers into fists. I breathe in, hold it, and then let out a whoosh of air. I'm determined.

I tried to remain calm.

I tried.

She won't get away with this.

2

KATELYN

I jerk awake. The room is dark, and for a moment a sharp spike of fear slides through me. I don't know where I am, until—

I heave a sigh of relief. I'm still at Luke's apartment. I remember falling asleep in his arms, feeling so safe and secure.

I reach toward him, and—

Where is he?

Probably in the bathroom. I look toward the door leading to the bathroom, but there's no sliver of light at the bottom. He probably just got up to go and didn't bother with the lights. Didn't want to wake me.

I draw in a deep breath, stretch my arms above my head. Relaxation swirls through me, and I close my eyes. I imagine myself lying on a beach, the sun streaming down on me, warming my body and my soul. In the distance the waves crash, and I feel at home.

So at home here with Luke.

Soon I'm asleep again.

3

LUKE

"Who the fuck are you?" I grit out.

"I'm the person who's going to take you back to LA so you can get what's coming to you."

"You're a damned bounty hunter? No fucking way." I begin to turn my head—

He forces the gun harder into my back.

Damn, he's not fooling around.

"Look, whatever they're paying you, I'll double it."

"Right."

I'm calm. Strike that. Not calm. My ability to stay calm vanished with the alcohol. I'm a fucking mess with a heart that's trying to pound right out of my chest, but I can at least act like I'm in control. I'd give my right arm for a drink.

No! I can't go there. Katelyn. This is all for Katelyn. I draw in a breath.

"I'm serious," I say. "If you know who I am, you know who my father is. I'll fucking double it."

He repositions the gun so it feels less like a broom handle digging into my spine...but only slightly less.

My heart is still racing, but at least he's thinking about my offer.

Fuck it all. I'm ready to head back, to pay my damned dues, and someone decides to put a bounty on my head.

"Put the gun down, man. I'm going to miss my bus."

"Lucifer Raven? On a bus?"

"You think I'm hanging out at a bus station in the middle of the night for my health?"

I heave a sigh of relief when the nose of the gun moves from my back. I've got my own piece strapped to my ankle, but I'm not in a position to get to it.

Still, I don't dare turn around.

"Who the hell are you?" I demand.

"Turn around and see."

I move slowly. He still has a gun trained on me, so I don't dare go for my ankle holster.

I don't look at his face at first. Hell, no. I need to know where the gun is.

Still in his right hand, and still pointed in my direction.

Okay, at least I know where it is. My hands are instinctively raised as I look up to his face.

A face I recognize.

A face I want to pummel.

"You've got to be fucking kidding me."

EMILY'S QUICK, *but she's not as quick as I am. I'm strong and fit— my job requires it. I have to be able to fight my way out of any situation, with or without weapons.*

By the time we're out of her cottage, I've got her in a stranglehold, my knife against the milky flesh of her neck.

"Why do you make me do this?" I whisper to her. "This isn't me."

"Please. Just leave me alone," she whimpers. "Let me be happy."

Let her be happy? She was happy back home. With me. I've done everything to make her happy, and she doesn't appreciate any of it.

"I'm happy here," she says. "Please, Lucifer."

"You will only be happy with me!" I whisper savagely, and I dig the blade into her neck without cutting her.

"No!" she screams. "Help me! Someone help me!"

"Damn it, Emily. Why?"

She continues screaming. I can't hurt her. I never want to hurt her. I love her. But if she doesn't stop screaming, what choice will I have?

Her screams bring security officers, as I knew they would.

I resist the niggling at the back of my neck. I could leave now. Let her go and hightail it out of here. I have the ability. You don't do what I do on a daily basis and not know how to make yourself invisible when you need to.

But letting her go...

Not a viable option. She's mine. She belongs to me and no one else.

More security surrounds us as spectators are shooed away.

"Put the knife down," one of the officers says. "Put it down and we'll talk. You don't come out of this alive if you don't."

"Fuck off!" I shout.

Emily goes more rigid against me. Something changed. Does she see someone? Someone who means something to her? The man whose shirt she's wearing?

The slithering anger snakes through me. I'll fucking end him.

"Emily!" A man's voice.

Emily shakes her head slightly. Is she communicating with him? Damn it!

"Emily!" The voice again, this time hoarser.

"Who is that?" I whisper. "Tell me who it is so I can end you both."

She shakes her head vehemently.

"Let her go!" Again the damned voice. "Take me instead!"

A security guard grabs a man—a dark-haired man wearing board shorts and no shirt.

The anger again. So much anger. So that's him. A fucking surfer boy. An island bum. Really, Emily?

The officer pulls him away, beyond where they've taped off the area. He paces around, raking his fingers through his hair.

"That?" I say to Emily. "That's who you're fucking?"

She doesn't respond. Still stays rigid. The blade knicks her skin slightly.

"Damn it," I say. "You've made me hurt you."

"You always hurt me, Lucifer," she says. "Always."

"No. You make me do this. You make me."

The island guy again, and he's mouthing words to her. I love you.

No fucking way. He can't have her. He can't have what's mine.

God, I need a drink—a fucking shitload of bourbon will get me through this. I think again about releasing her. I can still run, still get away.

"Let her go," an officer with a bullhorn shouts. "You hurt her, you go down."

"If I die, we both die!" I shout back.

Surfer boy runs then, crashes through the taped boundary, and—

A gunshot.

Fuck.

A gunshot.

Pain lances through me, but I hold steady. I hold steady... I hold steady...

But my brain has no more control over my body, and the knife... The knife... It falls from my grasp, tumbles to the ground.

In slow motion.

All in slow motion.

Emily runs away.

Away from me.

And I fall...into nothing.

4

KATELYN

I wake up to the warmth of the morning sun on my face. The light from Luke's lone window streams in, casting a luminescent veil over the small studio.

Instinctively, I reach for him.

Then I jerk upward. "Luke?"

The bathroom door is closed. He'll be out in a moment.

I crawl over to the edge of the bed and sit up.

And then I notice...

The suitcase—the suitcase that was sitting on his bed that he moved to the floor last night—is gone.

I stand, and it hits me. I woke up in the middle of the night. I woke up and he wasn't there.

No. I nearly run to the bathroom and pull the door open. "Luke?"

He's not standing at the sink.

He's not sitting on the toilet.

I throw back the shower curtain.

No Luke.

I open the mirrored cabinet above the sink. The bottle of hair color is gone, but he left his contact case and solution.

No big deal. He probably has travel sizes he uses. I grab the contact lens case and open it. I suck in a breath.

A pair of contacts sits inside the case. But they're not regular clear contact lenses.

They're brown. Colored lenses. Made to make eyes look brown.

"Oh, Luke..." I say aloud. "What have you done?"

My heart sinks and sadness sweeps through me.

He left.

Luke left without telling me.

My eyes glaze over, but I grab hold of the sink with both hands. No. I will *not* lose it. I've worked too hard to begin taking my life back.

I will not ruin it over any man.

Not even Luke Johnson.

Except that I love Luke Johnson.

How can I? How can I love a man so quickly? Especially after all I've been through?

I need a friend. I need to talk.

"Get a grip, Katelyn." The strength of my voice surprises even me. I close the mirror cabinet and face myself. My glassy eyes are front and center. I sniffle a little. "You will *not*," I say to my reflection, "lose what you've accomplished. You will *not*."

I take a quick shower, dress, and leave Luke's apartment, not bothering to even try to lock the door.

He left me here. Without so much as a note. If he gets robbed, I don't give a damn.

I catch a cab back to my place. Then my phone buzzes.

"Katelyn! It's Zee. Are you all right?"

Oh no. I promised Zee I'd let someone know if I were going to be gone all night again. One mistake after another.

"I'm so sorry. I should have called. I should have let security know."

"Katelyn, you're not in prison. You're not on parole. You don't have to check in. But we worry about you."

"I know that. I'm so, so sorry."

"I'm just glad you're okay."

"Trust me when I say this will never happen again."

"Don't make a promise you can't keep, Katelyn."

"Zee, I guarantee you I won't make this mistake again. Luke and I... Luke and I are over."

A pause. Then, "Oh... I'm sorry. Are you all right?"

"It was just too soon. You were right. Macy was right. Just too damned soon."

"What do you... Would you like to come see the baby today?"

"No, you haven't been home that long. I don't want to impose."

"You're the baby's godmother, Katelyn. It's not an imposition. I want you to meet her."

"All right. I'd love that."

"Where are you now?"

"I'm in a cab. On the way home."

"Okay. Why don't you come up for lunch? Reid and I would love to see you."

Reid. Until this moment I had forgotten that Reid Wolfe offered me a job as his assistant. I start Monday.

Good. I'll need something to take my mind off of Luke.

I never should have gotten involved with him in the first place.

Maybe all men suck.

Except that's not true. Reid doesn't suck.

I sigh into the phone. "I haven't had the chance to thank you for putting in a good word for me with Reid. I'm beyond humbled to be given a chance like this."

"I think you're going to do great, Katelyn," Zee says.

"I know you kind of feel responsible for me."

"I feel responsible for all of you, but you are the one I chose to work with Reid. You're smart, Katelyn. Anyone who meets you knows it. It's not your fault you didn't get to go to college and follow the path you wanted to."

"Zee…"

"This isn't pity. This is just a helping hand. I'm in a position to help, and I want to do it. When I've done all I can do, the rest is up to you."

"I know. You're right."

"Good. We'll see you soon."

After ending the call, I think about Zee's words.

This isn't pity, Katelyn.

Pity.

How I hate the word.

I've been determined, through everything, not to succumb to self-pity. My God, I went through hell on that island. Ten years of being held captive and being forced to serve men in their depraved fetishes.

And through all of it? Never once did I feel self-pity.

And through all the hard work to get over it? I still didn't feel self-pity.

So why am I feeling it now?

A guy walked out on me. I'm certainly not the first woman to get jilted.

No.

I will not succumb to self-pity.

Except...

Tears are rolling down my cheeks. I'm sniffling. Even trembling a bit.

And before I know it...

I'm sobbing.

I cry and I cry and I cry. Loud gasping sobs, and I'm not sure how to stop them.

5

LUKE

I'm expecting someone from my past—someone who has reason to want me to pay.

Reason to want me dead.

What I'm not expecting is—

Those fucking yellow eyes—the eyes I first saw at The Glass House, when this man was stalking Katelyn.

"What the hell is your name again? Pollack?"

"I knew something was off about you the first time I saw you," Pollack says. "Now, you're going to take me to Moonstone."

"What the hell are you talking about?"

"Moonstone. You call her Katelyn."

Anger rises in me. Anger.

God, the anger.

But it's different this time. It's stronger—stronger because I love Katelyn.

I love her more than Emily. More than all the others.

I'm willing to die for her to be worthy of her.

So I left.

What was I thinking? I can't leave Katelyn. I need to protect her.

Luke Johnson doesn't have any means to protect Katelyn.

But Lucifer Raven?

The old Lucifer Raven, at least, could protect her. Lucifer Raven now? More people want him dead than alive.

The only thing that's true is that I can't leave. Not without Katelyn. Or at least not without knowing she's safe.

With a swift roundhouse kick, I disarm Pollack. Then within another two seconds, my own piece is out of my ankle strap and pointed toward his heart.

"You're going to be very sorry you messed with me," I tell him through gritted teeth. "Clearly, you know my real name, but you obviously know little else."

His hands go up in the air. "Hey, it's all good. I'm sorry. I'll leave her alone."

"Yeah, and I'm supposed to take your word for that? You're sick. You're one of those fucking degenerates who messed with her on that island."

"If that's what I was, I'd be in prison now."

"You'd think, wouldn't you? But I know how easy it is to avoid prison, even when you've done reprehensible things."

He widens his eyes, and his lips quiver.

"You're right about one thing. I *am* Lucifer Raven, but I'm betting you don't know how powerful I am, or my actual identity."

"You're a drug dealer. From LA."

"You think so? Is that all you know?"

"I…"

"Just as I suspected. You may know my alias, but you don't know exactly who I am."

"All I know is that if I tell Katelyn who you are, she'll go running."

"You think she'll believe you after what you've done to her?"

No reply. Not that I expect one. I'm right on target, and we both know it.

"Here's what's going to happen," I say. "You're going to stay the hell away from Katelyn. Because if you don't, I will make sure you pay in the worst possible way for what you did to her on that island."

"Wait—"

I shake my head. "You're done talking. You're going to show me where you live, what you're doing here, and then you're going to tell me exactly how you avoided prison. Is that fucking clear?"

He nods slightly, his lips still quivering.

"You've made me miss my bus, asshole, so now we're going to your place."

POLLOCK LIVES in a studio not unlike my own. I sit in a chair, my gun still trained on him.

"Start talking."

"This remains between you and me," he says.

"You really think you're in a position to make deals?"

He looks down at his lap. "I'm not proud of what I've done."

"Right. I've got some alligator land in Florida I'd like to sell you, too."

"I'm serious." He lifts his head, but he doesn't quite meet

my gaze. "I... I gave the FBI information in exchange for immunity."

"I see. And is that what you're not proud of? Or is it the fact that you tortured Katelyn on that island?"

"All of it."

"Why did you get immunity? What did you do to convince the Feds that you should have the right to walk around society?"

"I never touched her."

My God, I could murder this degenerate with my bare hands. That anger... That slithering anger...

So much harsher than before.

I steel myself. "Again...let's talk about that alligator land in the swamp."

"I'm serious," he says. "I never touched her. I swear to God."

"So you went to a tropical island—a known hunting ground—where millionaires of your ilk got to pay to hunt women, to rape women, to torture women, and you're telling me you never touched Katelyn."

"That is exactly what I'm telling you. If you are who you say you are, you know the FBI would not give immunity to someone who was a risk."

"What did you do to her, then? Katelyn obviously hates you. What the fuck did you do to her?"

He sinks his head down, his chin touching his chest.

"I'm waiting. Again, if you know who I am, you know I will not have a problem pulling this trigger."

He lifts his head with a gasp. "Have you...killed before?"

"We're not talking about me, dickhead. We're talking about you. Katelyn hates you. You scare the hell out of her. Now you tell me... What the fuck did you do to her?"

"I... I can't talk about this."

"You'd better start."

He remains silent, and part of me is okay with that. I'm not sure I want to hear what he did to Katelyn. If he truly never hurt her in the physical sense, then what he did must have been emotional abuse, mental abuse.

Sometimes that can be worse. I should know.

"I'm ageing here, shithead."

He looks up, again not meeting my gaze. Best I can tell he's staring at the wall above me.

"I have issues."

"Don't we all. Cry me a fucking river."

"I... I can't tell you what I did. I just can't. But I will tell you that I never harmed her."

"You clearly did."

"Perhaps, but not in the way you think."

"Mental abuse is still abuse."

"I—"

"Whatever you did to her, you obviously did without her consent."

Again...silence.

And again, it occurs to me that I'm not sure I want to know what he did to her. If he actually says it, I may pull this fucking trigger.

If I do that, my life is effectively over.

Hell, it's probably over anyway. Once I get back to LA, try to make things right, someone will kill me.

This slug of a human being isn't worth my life. But he's worth Katelyn's life. Of course, if I shoot him, I'll be dragged off to prison, and I won't be here to protect Katelyn.

"Katelyn obviously means enough to you that you came after me. That you researched me and found out who I was."

No reply.

"How did you find out?"

"I can't reveal my sources."

"You seem to keep forgetting who's holding the gun."

"They'll kill me."

"And do you think I won't?"

"I'm thinking that if you were going to, you already would have."

He's not wrong.

Man, I need to up my game. I've only been Luke Johnson for less than a year, but already, part of Lucifer Raven is gone.

That's not a bad thing. It's what I was after in the first place. But if I'm going to protect Katelyn, I have to be Lucifer Raven. I have to remember how to deal with this kind of shit.

I move toward him and place the nose of the pistol right at his temple.

He trembles. "Please..."

"Please what?"

"Please...don't kill me."

"You have no idea who you're dealing with. You have no idea what you're doing."

"It's Moonstone. She makes me do...ridiculous things. I... I love her."

I scoff. "You don't fucking love her. You don't even know what love is."

My own words aren't lost on me. Do *I* even know what love is? I abused the women I professed to love in my previous life. I never meant to. But I made excuses for myself. I told them they were the reason I was hurting them.

Therapy proved me wrong. Getting off alcohol proved me wrong as well.

But I wonder... Are Pollack and I that different?

He claims to love Katelyn, but I know he hurt her. She wouldn't be frightened of him if he hadn't.

Will I ever be worthy of her?

I thought if I returned to LA, dealt with what I left behind, perhaps I would be.

Even if I died, at least I would die worthy of the woman I love.

But now...

I look at Pollack...and I may as well be looking in the fucking mirror.

6

KATELYN

Nearly an hour later I can finally breathe without gasping.

I can finally look at myself without bursting into tears again.

But oh my God...my face. My nose is red and swollen, my eyelids nearly double their normal size and also red. The whites of my eyes are bloodshot.

No way will I look decent for my lunch at Zee and Reid's place.

I grab my phone to cancel when it buzzes.

"Hello?"

"Katelyn, baby. It's Luke."

My heart swells. "Luke! Where are you? Are you all right?"

"I'm fine. And...I'm sorry."

Thank God. I sigh in relief. "I'm just glad you're okay."

Should I be angry? I can't be. Not yet. Not now.

"I'm sorry for leaving you at my place."

"What happened?"

"You know I had plans to leave for a while. The plans have been put on hold."

Thank God again. I shouldn't be so needy, but the thought of being without Luke... I can't fathom it. "When can I see you?"

"I'm not sure. I have some stuff to take care of."

"Luke..."

"Katelyn, I love you. That hasn't changed. But there are some things... Things you don't know about me."

"There are things you don't know about me either."

He pauses a moment. "Maybe we don't need to know everything about each other, but I do need you to tell me one thing."

"Anything," I say. "I'll tell you anything."

"The guy from the restaurant—Pollack. I need to know what he did to you."

Anything but that.

I swallow. How can I tell Luke the truth? How can I tell him what the asshole—Mr. Smith, Ice Man—did to me?

It's so humiliating.

Ice Man.

I can't speak. It's too difficult. I love Luke too much. I can't let him bear this with me.

"Baby...?"

"Luke, please understand. I don't want to relive any of that."

"Katelyn, I need to know. He approached me, held a gun to me, wanted me to bring him to you."

I suck in a breath. No. Just no. I can't go back there. Just can't.

"Don't worry. I won't let him get anywhere near you. But he claims he never harmed you."

"That's not true."

"I know it's not true. But he's out walking for some reason, which means he must have been able to convince someone in high places that he wasn't a threat to society."

"He's a threat to *me*."

"I need you to do something for me, then. If you won't tell me what he did to you, I need you to talk to a lawyer about a restraining order."

"I don't know any lawyers."

"The Wolfes know a lot of lawyers. They'll be able to help you get a restraining order."

"Can *you* help me?"

He sighs. "Baby, I wish I could. I don't have any connections like that."

"I understand."

It's not a lie. I do understand. But there are things that Luke isn't telling me. No one disappears in the middle of the night if they're not hiding something.

"Luke?"

"Yeah?"

"Promise me you won't leave me."

Silence greets me on the other end of the line.

"Luke?"

"Katelyn, I love you. I will always love you. Which is why I won't make a promise to you that I'm not sure I can keep."

Knife in heart. Heart in stomach. Luke. I need him. I hate that I need him, but I do.

"What's going on? Please. You know almost everything about me. You can tell me."

Silence.

I won't force him to talk to me. I can't do that. After all, I just refused to tell him what Ice Man did to me. Forcing him to talk to me when I won't talk to him isn't fair.

"Baby, just remember how much I love you."

"That goes both ways, Luke. You need to remember how much I love you. How much I need you. How much I don't want you to leave."

Another heavy sigh meets my ears. "I do understand. I can't promise I'm going to be here forever, sweetie. I wish I could, but I can't."

"What are you hiding?"

And again, more silence.

"Can you get me an audience?" he asks finally. "With Reid Wolfe?"

"I can try."

"Okay. And if you can't, that's okay too."

"When will I see you?"

"I'm not sure, baby. Maybe tonight. I'll text you if it's possible."

"Okay. I love you, Luke."

"I love you too, Katelyn. Always."

The call ends, but I keep the phone in my ear, as if it's my last lifeline to Luke.

All the sobbing... I thought he had left me. Indeed he did. But something brought him back. Was it Pollack?

Why all the questions about Pollack? Luke knows the kind of things that went on at that island. But Pollock was unique. No, he didn't physically touch me. Unless you count with his urine stream.

But he was my least favorite of all the men who visited me there.

Lovebird used to beat me.

Broomstick would sodomize me with a broom handle.

And Camouflage...

Camouflage liked to hunt me.

He was hardly alone. A lot of them liked to beat me and rape me and even hunt me.

But Camouflage took hunting to a new level.

Then...the time they all descended on me... When I became Moonstone...

Moonstone saved me from all of them except Ice Man.

"No!" I finally move the phone from my ear and throw it against the wall.

I can't. I can't go back there.

And it dawns on me then.

Yes, I'm humiliated, and yes, it's embarrassing to tell Luke what Ice Man did to me.

But the real reason is that I cannot bear to say the words. I've said them in therapy so many times, and now...I just can't.

I'm trying to take back my life, and if I dwell on what happened to me, I won't be able to do that.

I'm not blocking it out. Far from it.

But I can't talk about it anymore. Especially not to Luke. I want our life together to be perfect. We're in love, and I can't let anything damage that.

I head to the bathroom and wash my face, tempted to scrub the redness away, but that will only make it worse. Instead, I let the water run until it's ice cold and then I rinse my face ten times. Ten more times.

Next, some eye drops take care of the redness.

But my nose and eyes are still swollen. Not much I can do about that.

And it's time to go over to Zee's place. To that horrid building.

It's okay. I can handle it. I went for the interview, and I can go to visit baby Honor.

I try a little bit of makeup, but it only makes me look worse. I dab it all away with a cotton ball and makeup remover. I change my clothes. Black leggings and a pink tunic. Not my best look, but it will have to do.

I lock up and go downstairs to hail a cab.

Time to buck up. To face life.

Always. I will *not* let the bastards grind me down.

7

LUKE

"She wouldn't tell me," I say to Pollock, "so you're going to."

"No."

I drop my gaze to my pistol sitting in my lap. "I don't need to remind you about the gun."

"I can't." His cheeks are red.

"Embarrassed, are you?"

"It's not me. There were just things that... The island made me do it."

"Right. You're not responsible for your own actions."

Again, the similarities between us are not lost on me.

The fact that I could be looking at myself angers me. Pollack is a degenerate, but was I anything less before I got help? Before I escaped the life I made for *my*self?

"I could use a fucking drink," Pollack says.

"Excuse me?"

"Sorry. I could just use a damned drink."

"No."

"Are you sure? I've got some good shit."

"I don't fucking drink, asshole."

"Oh."

"And if you think I'm going to play bartender for you while I hold my gun on you, think again."

Pollack rubs his forehead. "Fine. You win. I'll stay away from her."

"Damn right you will, and if you're not going to tell me what you did to her, I'm going to assume the worst. And if you know anything about me, you know I can make sure that you're punished appropriately."

He visibly shudders once more. I wonder if he's pissing his pants, he looks so scared.

"Fine. What are you going to do to me?"

"The fact that you went to all the trouble to find out who I actually was shows me that Katelyn is important to you. Degenerates like you don't have normal emotions, so I'm thinking you're obsessed with her, which means I can tell you to stay away from her all day. I can get a restraining order against you. But if I'm right, you will continue to stalk her. Because you're obsessed."

"I'm not. I'm seriously not."

"Talk is cheap, Pollack. You researched me, got information that you probably shouldn't have gotten from any source that I know of, and you found me and held me at gunpoint demanding that I take you to her. You're obsessed, all right. So obsessed that you don't know how deep you're in."

"Who the hell *are* you, man?"

"I'm your worst fucking nightmare, asshole. And I'm not even close to exaggerating."

He shudders and seems to sink into his chair.

I look around his small place, which is even smaller than my own. He's certainly not living in the lap of luxury. Is he in a witness protection program? If that's the case, what is he doing having dinner at The Glass House?

Someone is helping him.

Or...he's just that rich. I don't know a lot about Derek Wolfe's Treasure Island, but I do know it cost over a million dollars a day to go there.

It may have cost more to take part in the extracurricular activities.

I don't know.

But...

A man sits across from me who *does* know. He'll tell me what he did to Katelyn. I have no doubt about that. All I've done so far is threaten to blow his head off. I'm no stranger to inflicting torture, and he *will* tell me what I want to know.

But first I'm going to get some general information about the island.

How much it cost to go there, and who else was there.

"I know what you people did to the women on that island. I know you treated them like animals, and once you caught them, you could do whatever you wanted to them, save kill them. You sit here and tell me you didn't do any physical harm to Katelyn. Maybe you're not lying. If you had done physical harm to any woman on that island, I doubt you'd be walking around a free man. Which means you did something horrible to her, something you're embarrassed to tell me. Even when I have a gun pointing at your head. So basically all I can ascertain from that is that you are some psycho freak, Pollack. And I don't like thinking about some psycho freak anywhere near Katelyn."

"She doesn't seem like a Katelyn to me," he says. "She'll always be Moonstone."

"Why do you call her Moonstone?"

"All the women—they had names of gemstones. She was called Moonstone, probably because of her light blue eyes, her blond hair, her fair skin."

What does a moonstone even look like? Katelyn is a diamond, for sure. The rarest, clearest diamond ever.

"Her name is Katelyn," I say through gritted teeth. "She was never Moonstone. I don't care what they called her on that island. The person on that island was not her. She was held there against her will, you sick freak."

"You think I don't know that? I'm in love with her, for God's sake."

My jaw drops. "You? Happily married man that you are?"

I drop my gaze to his left hand. He's still wearing the fake wedding band he wore when he accosted Katelyn at The Glass House.

"I'm a married man." Pollack holds up his left hand, displaying a gawdy thick gold band. *"I just thought this woman was a friend of my daughter's. I can see now I'm mistaken."*

Right. He's married. This tiny studio shows no sign of any woman living here. And he thinks he's in love with Katelyn? Seriously?

"You don't know what love is."

Again, though, my past filters through my mind. The times I thought I was in love with Emily and the others. I wasn't in love with any of them. I was in love *at* them. In love with the *control*. And again, as I look at Pollock—his tired face, his receding hairline, his damned yellow eyes—part of me sees familiarity. Physically we have no resemblance to each other whatsoever, but I was once a man who treated women poorly.

Are we even that different?

I suppress a shudder that wants to run through my body

and turn me to ice. I didn't hunt women. I didn't torture or rape them. But I did strike them on occasion. I did keep them locked up.

I told myself it was for their own safety, and that the punishment was necessary for their disobedience.

I convinced myself that they made me do it.

God, I was fucked up.

I don't deserve Katelyn now, and I may never. The only way I can possibly hope to is if I go back to LA and make amends as best I can.

Which will undoubtedly end in my death.

Pollack rings his hands together. "Just kill me. Kill me now and get it over with. I can't live like this any longer. If I can't have Moonstone, I'll die anyway."

"Don't give me that pity party bullshit," I say. "I don't buy it now, and I won't ever buy it. You did some kind of heinous thing to my woman, and the only reason you're not dead now is because there's more information I want to get out of you."

I won't kill Pollack. I've never killed another person. I've hired it out, but never actually pulled the trigger myself. Does that make me any less guilty?

No, not really. Just like Pollack is no less guilty even if he didn't physically harm Katelyn.

Fuck. What was I thinking, believing I could live a normal life? Believing I could truly escape my past? Believing I could be Luke Johnson, no man and every man?

I train my gun on him once more. "You're going to tell me, and you're going to tell me now. What did you pay to go to that island? Who are the others who went there? And where are they now?"

8

KATELYN

Even though I was recently here for my interview with Reid, this building still gives me the creeps.

Somewhere, in the depths, underground, I was hunted, tortured, starved, my shoulders dislocated.

Zee.

The place where I first met Zee.

I can handle this. I must. Part of taking back my life is taking back the places that haunt me.

Though this is the Wolfe office building, both Reid and his brother Rock live here on the top floors. After going through the requisite security and checking in with reception, I head up on their private elevator accompanied by a security guard.

At least I know I'm safe here. They have just as much security here as they do at my apartment complex.

The elevator opens right into Zee's penthouse.

"Go on in," the guard says. "The housekeeper will take you to Mrs. Wolfe."

A woman greets me. "Hello, Ms. Brooks. I'm Lydia. Mrs.

Wolfe is waiting for you in the nursery." She leads me through a large living area to a hallway and then to an open door.

Zee sits in a rocking chair, a tiny bundle in her arms. She looks up and smiles. But it quickly turns to a frown.

"Katelyn, what happened?"

My hands instinctively go to my cheeks. My swollen eyes, my red nose. The housekeeper and the security guard didn't say anything, but of course they wouldn't. They're paid for their silence, to mind their own business.

"I'm fine."

"You're not fine. You've been crying."

"Actually...Luke called me. He didn't leave town after all."

"That's good. Why the crying?"

"I did the crying before I knew that."

Zee smiles weakly. She knows, as well as I do, that I probably shouldn't be pursuing a relationship right now anyway. It's just too soon.

But I fell in love. I fell in love quickly and passionately and now... Now I don't know how to live without Luke.

Ugh. I don't even like the thought. I've gotten through hell, and now I let the fact that my man might've left me send me into a tailspin.

I'm *not* going to be that woman.

"Enough about me," I say. "I came here to see your beautiful baby." I lean down.

Honor is sleeping, her tiny eyes closed. Her features are fine. Of course she'll be beautiful. She's Zee and Reid's child. But for a newborn, she is extraordinarily stunning with fine black hair, a tiny button nose, and full pink lips.

"She's breathtaking, Zee."

"She is, isn't she? But I admit to being biased."

"Of course you're biased. You made her. But she truly is gorgeous."

Zee traces Honor's tiny lips with her finger. "I can't get enough of her. I absolutely can't stop looking at her. I have to force myself not to pick her up when she's sleeping soundly because I just never want to let her go."

I nod, smiling. Will I ever have a baby? A long time ago, before the island, I used to think I wanted children. Now? I'm not sure I'm whole enough. Sure, I have my strength. Sure, I'm determined to take my life back.

A child, though... A child deserves so much more than a mother who's been broken.

But perhaps I'm not beyond repair. Perhaps one day I can have a baby who is as beautiful to me as Honor is to Zee.

"This is your Auntie Katelyn, Nora," Zee says in a hushed voice.

"Don't wake her," I say.

"I won't, but I wish she would open her eyes so you could see them. They're blue, just like Reid's. Dark blue."

"Don't all babies have blue eyes?"

"I thought that too," she says. "Turns out it's an old wives' tale. Of course, since both Reid and I have blue eyes, Nora's fate was sealed."

"She's already beautiful," I say.

"Thank you. Would you like to hold her?"

Something jumps in my belly, as if my uterus is skipping a beat. "I don't want to wake her."

"It's okay." Zee stands, and she carefully hands Nora to me.

My God, my uterus beats again. I know I'm imagining it, but holding this beautiful little human in my hands, I feel like I can handle anything.

"I can't even express how much I feel right now," I say.

"Have you held a baby before?"

"No. I haven't. I never did any babysitting for newborns. Only older children. And then of course..."

"I know. The island."

"It all comes back to that, doesn't it?"

"No," she says. "It *doesn't* all come back to that. Granted, I never made it to the island, but you *can* heal, Katelyn. And you're already doing so well. The best of everyone, according to the counselors at the retreat center and to Macy as well."

"Macy gives you reports?"

"Just in general. She would never violate the doctor-patient privilege."

"Oh, no, I'm not worried about that. I just..."

"What?"

"I don't know. Sometimes I think I've got this, you know? I think I'm strong and there's nothing I can't do. But then other times... Like this morning, for example. When I thought Luke had left me, I broke down. I broke down so hard."

"I know you did."

My cheeks warm. It's no secret, given what my face looks like at the moment.

"It's okay, Katelyn. There will be good days and bad days. Hell, there will be good minutes and bad minutes, and they can happen within a second of each other. Believe me. I haven't been through what you've been through, but I do understand."

Besides the other women from the island, Zee is truly the only other person who gets it.

"Have you gotten together with any of the other girls?"

"Only Lily and Aspen are here so far. Oh...and Kelly."

"Do you feel like you could be friends with any of them?"

"I don't know. I suppose it's strange. We were all on the island together. We all lived in the same dorm. But I don't really feel that we were ever friends."

"I understand."

Does she, though? When we were in the dorm, we didn't talk about what happened on the island. The dorm was our only refuge. The men weren't allowed there, so the last thing we wanted was to be reminded of the island, and the other women reminded us of it. So most of us stayed quiet. Every once in a while I'd see a few of the girls talking, but I was never one of them.

"Maybe I'll try. It would be nice to have a friend."

"You have me. I'm not going anywhere. But I agree with you. You need more than one friend."

Especially when my one friend has a new husband and a new baby taking up her time. And college classes on top of that.

"You're absolutely right. I'll try. Maybe Aspen. Kelly... She's still running, and Lily... I don't know."

"Sometimes you feel a connection and sometimes you don't. If you feel you and Aspen might get along and be friends, start with her. If that doesn't work out, Lily and Kelly are there. And give Kelly a chance. As you know, none of this is easy."

I nod, staring down at Nora's sweet little lips. Absently, I trace them with my finger as I watched Zee do earlier.

"Perfect, isn't she?" Zee says. "Like a little China doll."

"She is. She totally is."

Already the tears begin falling again.

9

LUKE

"The cost depended on the season. I didn't have as much money as a lot of the others, so I came on the off-season. Summer, usually. The cost was one point two million per day."

"What the fuck do you do that you could afford that?"

"I inherited my money. From a great aunt who didn't have any other relatives."

"You inherited enough money from some old bat so that you could afford one point two million per day to go to a tropical island and hunt women."

"I didn't say I was proud of it. I've got nothing now. Part of my deal was that I paid a huge-ass fine."

That explains his humble lodging. "What a piece of work," I say more to myself than to him.

But again, I wonder... Are we all that different?

My old man could probably have afforded the place. Did he ever go there? His net worth is close to a billion, but he's not nearly as rich as the Wolfes. He's a producer in LA, but that's not what made him rich. He comes from old money, not like Derek Wolfe who was pretty much a self-made man. As far as I know, anyway.

"Who else went there?"

"We all signed nondisclosure agreements. Some of them wore masks or otherwise altered their appearance."

"Don't care. You're going to tell me who was there."

"I...can't."

"Bullshit. There's a reason you're not rotting in a prison cell, and I'm betting that you didn't get off with just that huge-ass fine. You turned evidence."

He looks down at his lap.

Bingo.

"Start talking."

"Can you guarantee my safety?"

"Are you kidding me? I've got a gun pointed at you, and you're asking me to guarantee your safety?"

His lips tremble again. "If you were going to kill me, you would've already done it."

"Clearly you don't know how this works," I say. "I want information. You can't give me information if you're dead, so I'll get the information first."

I have no intention of killing the bastard, but what he doesn't know won't hurt him.

I repeat the serenity prayer inside my mind.

God, grant me the serenity to accept the things I cannot change, the courage to change the things I can, and the wisdom to know the difference.

I must stay focused. I can't let the rage I used to feel consume me once more.

And damn, it's hard. This man did something horrible to Katelyn, and for that reason alone I could kill him with my bare hands.

Yes, my rage was fueled by alcohol. But it was also a part of me that I have to work to keep at bay.

One high-profile person who frequented the island made the news. Prince Christian of Cordova, a small principality off the southern coast of France. Their only claim to fame is their royal family, whose pictures always grace the tabloids.

Prince Christian was the heir apparent, but now that title has passed to his sister Princess Salome.

"Did you ever meet Prince Christian?" I ask.

"No. He was never there when I was."

"Who was there? When you were there?"

He keeps his lips pressed shut.

"Get talking. I don't have a lot of patience left. You can tell me now or you can tell me later when I'm gutting you."

"I wish I could."

"Damn it, that nondisclosure agreement means nothing right now. It was illegal when you signed it because you were on an island doing illegal activities."

"It was a private island. Who's to say what the law was?"

"You can't be talking serious. You and everyone else who visited that island knew exactly what you were doing, and you knew exactly how wrong it was. Now start talking, or I swear to God I will cut you but I will keep you alive so you can tell me what I want to know."

"You can't—" he gasps.

I'm holding a knife now. I pulled it out of the band of my ankle holster. It glitters even in the artificial light of the studio, and the steel blade is sharp enough to break skin at first contact.

I've had this knife for years. My old man gave it to me. I used one like it on the island myself, when I tried to get Emily to come back to me. That one I stole from one of the island security guards.

Yes, I know what I'm doing. I'm skilled in weapon and unarmed combat.

"Have you ever gutted a bird, Mr. Pollack?"

He shakes his head while shivering.

"Gutting an animal's not that different. My father used to hunt wild game in Africa. Cost him an arm and a leg, but he loved doing it. I never acquired the taste for it myself, but he used to drag me along with him anyway, make me watch as he gutted those poor animals simply for their pelts."

I'm lying. My father never hunted wild game in his life. Neither did I. I have no desire to. I love animals.

But the lie is working. Pollack's face is twisted with terror. He's beyond frightened at this point.

He's petrified. Completely and utterly petrified.

"Okay, okay..." He rattles off five names I recognize. All rich men, all well known.

None of whom are in prison right now.

"Why weren't any of these people caught?"

"I don't know. Payoffs?"

He's probably right. "Those are the names you gave the Feds?"

He nods, still shaking.

"Yet none of those fuckers are in prison."

"Plenty of them are, I heard."

"Not the ones you just named."

"Yeah, but those are the big names. These people can buy their way out of any kind of mess."

"Can they?"

My question is rhetorical, of course. My old man can buy

his way out of anything. Hell, he bought my freedom. Which has turned out to be short-lived.

If a bozo like Pollack can find out who I am, can't anyone?

Of course, he may have found my alias, but he doesn't know who I am.

"There are a few others," he says. "That tech guy, Carlos Neptune. And then the blue-blood guy from California. He's a producer. Lucifer Ashton."

My blood runs cold.

My old man? My fucking old man?

If he touched Katelyn, I will *kill* him.

"Ashton's not in prison either," I say dryly.

"Like I said, money talks."

"How is Prince Christian incarcerated but not these wealthy Americans?"

"Because wealthy Americans can buy their freedom."

"So in addition to buying your freedom with Auntie's money, you're also a damned canary."

He doesn't say anything, but he doesn't have to. We both know the truth.

I'm as much of a canary as he is.

Again…I feel like I'm looking in a mirror.

What makes us so different?

And my father…

I always knew he was an asshole, but this?

Then again, I've watched him mistreat my mother my whole life. I grew up thinking that was the way one treated women, which was part of the reason why I was so hard on my girlfriends. Why I wanted to control them, order them around, punish them when they disobeyed me.

My God, no wonder I'm so fucked up.

10

KATELYN

I lift my hand, ready to knock on Aspen's door. She lives on the same floor. This building must be mostly vacant.

What's stopping me? I'm a little worried, feeling kind of shy.

But Zee is right. I need friends, and these women know more than anyone else what I've been through.

My fist comes down on the wooden door.

I knock once and then again.

I steer clear of the doorbell and the buzzer. A knock seems more friendly.

"Moonstone— I mean...Katelyn," Aspen says through the door.

"Hi, Aspen. I was just wondering if you wanted to get some coffee or something."

She opens the door. Aspen is beautiful with dark hair and eyes and fair skin. She's tall, muscular, and athletic. She was a professional volleyball player before...

And she was hunted viciously. Because of her athleticism,

some of the more degenerate visitors to the island liked to hunt her. She was a challenge.

To see her now, I wouldn't even know she had been on the island. She's not scarred, at least nowhere I can see. Diamond took such good care of all of us that we have fewer scars than we probably should have.

Aspen still hasn't answered my question.

Do I ask again? It's like I've forgotten how to be social.

"You know what?" Aspen finally says. "Yeah. Let's get the hell out of here for a little while."

We go downstairs, let security know we're going to take some time for coffee, and then we head out into the busy Manhattan streets. There is no dearth of coffee shops, so we choose the first one we find, which is only a couple buildings away.

I order a cinnamon mocha latte, and Aspen orders black coffee. Then we find a table by the window.

I open my mouth...but I have no idea what to say. Sheesh. This was my idea. I can't expect Aspen to start talking.

But thankfully, she does. "What's going on with you? Have you seen your family?"

"I've talked to them. They live in LA."

She drops her jaw. "Then why are you here?"

It's a valid question. "My family isn't what I need right now." No lie there.

"I get it."

"Wait. Aren't you from Colorado?"

"Yeah."

"So you're not with your family either."

"They're here, actually. My mom and dad rented an apartment for a few months. She takes a sip of her coffee. "It's a little...awkward."

"I can imagine. Part of the big reason why I'm here instead of LA. Plus, the Wolfes are helping us out so much and they're here."

She nods. "Don't get me wrong. My family is great and all. But they just... They don't understand, and I'm really *glad* they don't understand. I mean I wouldn't wish this on my worst enemy."

I consider her words. *My worst enemy.* I'm not so sure I agree with Aspen. My cousins Jared and Tony? The two who sold me off to that damned place? Jared is already dead, but Tony? He's rotting in a prison cell, but is that good enough for what he put me through? How many other women did they give to that priest?

I should try to find out.

Then again, should I?

This is all about reclaiming my life. Does reclaiming your life mean getting back at the person who put you in the position? Does it mean investigating and finding out who else that person hurt?

If they sent anyone else to that island, those girls are either dead or free now.

Dead.

How is this the first time I considered the word?

There were women who...

"Aspen," I say. "Do you remember Turquoise?"

"I have limited memory of my time on the island," she says. "All the therapists say it's a defense mechanism. They've offered me guided hypnosis to recover the memories, but why would I want to remember any of that?"

"I don't know. So you can work through it, maybe?"

"The reason I'm here is because I worked through as much of it as I could on the island. I'm in a fairly good headspace now. I know, that sounds ridiculous, doesn't it? I mean I was held captive for God knows how long."

"You don't remember how long you were there?"

"No, not really. Like I said, it's kind of a blank."

"But you know. Because you remember when you were taken."

"Yeah. I guess it's been about five years. I was taken from a hotel room during a tour with the team."

"Were any of the other team members taken?"

"No. I was the only lucky one," she says dryly.

Her beauty. Aspen's beauty made her a target.

"Is that why you're not wearing any makeup?"

"Yeah, it's also why I cut all my hair off."

Aspen is still gorgeous with short hair. There's no way to make her not gorgeous. She doesn't even need makeup. She's got that fresh-faced look of an athlete.

"I understand. It's like we no longer want to be noticed."

"That's it in a nutshell."

"Except that… I met someone."

Her eyes pop open. "Seriously?"

"Yeah, he's a server at The Glass House. Really nice guy. Even *I* can't believe what I'm feeling. Honestly, Aspen, I didn't think I'd ever have these feelings again."

"I know *I'll* never have those feelings again," she says. "I don't care if Hugh Jackman himself walks up to this table and propositions me."

I nod. I totally get where she's coming from. "Except Luke is way cuter than Hugh Jackman."

She laughs. "Totally not possible."

I take a few more drinks of my latte. "I'm not sure I'm ready. Can you tell I had a sobbing spree earlier today?"

"Not before you just mentioned it. But yeah, your eyes are slightly swollen."

"Believe me, they look a lot better than they did."

"So why the crying spree?"

I fill her in quickly.

"He didn't leave town after all?"

"Nope. So apparently I went on the crying jag for no reason."

"Have you considered that maybe…"

"What?"

"Maybe…you're just not ready."

"I've considered that from the moment this started. Believe me, it's in the forefront of my mind at all times. But I fell fast, and I fell hard. And you know what? It's pretty amazing. It's pretty amazing that I can feel anything, Aspen."

She nods, but in her eyes I see the truth. She's not buying it.

"You may be surprised," I tell her. "You may be able to feel something after all."

"Not going to happen. If the thought of Hugh Jackman can't get me moving, nothing can."

"I can't get Hugh Jackman for you," I say. "He's been married for like for*ever*, but don't sell yourself short. I believe in you. I believe in all of us."

"You sound like Macy."

"You weren't at group the other day," I say. "But Macy said something that really stuck with me."

"Oh?"

"Yeah. She said you don't have to wait until life is no longer difficult to be happy."

Aspen doesn't reply. She stares at her coffee cup, which is now empty.

"You want another?" I ask.

She shakes her head.

I still have a little bit of my latte left, so I finish quickly. "You've had enough social hour, haven't you?"

"Yeah," she says. "Is it that obvious?"

"I didn't mean to put you on the spot. I just wanted to... Hell, I don't know what I wanted to do. I guess I just wanted a friend."

She smiles then. "Okay, you've got one, then. But is it okay if we have different feelings about different things?"

"Of course it is. What would life be without different opinions? Pretty boring."

She nods. "Maybe I'll have another coffee after all."

11

___

LUKE

W hat do I do with this degenerate now?

As much as I want to make him pay with my bare hands—or with my knife or my gun—I can't go back to that place.

Damn... I want a drink.

Pollack has alcohol here.

He admitted it. I could easily go into his kitchen and find the booze. Just a sip. A sip would take the edge off.

One sip wouldn't send me back down the hole.

Except one sip *is* all it would take. Fuck, alcoholism is hard.

My muscles tense, and my thighs are ready to take me into a stand, walk me to the kitchen.

It's body versus brain.

Which will win out?

My body is craving alcohol right now, craving it as if I'm starving on a desert island.

Man... Almost craving it the way I crave Katelyn.

"You look like you could use a drink, man," Pollack says.

Fuck it all. Does he read minds now?

My fingers tighten around the gun. "Shut the fuck up, asshole."

"Easy... You just look a little tense."

Tense? I wish for tense. This is so beyond tense that I may shatter into pieces if I so much as move.

"So what do I do with you now?"

"Let me go?" He lets out a nervous chuckle.

"Yeah, *that's* going to happen."

Seriously, though, what *do* I do with him now? If I let him go, the first thing he'll do is call the cops on me. I can't have that because I need to get to LA and take care of things. I have a lot of red on my ledger, and I can't be worthy of Katelyn until I erase it.

Which will probably also mean erasing my life.

What I need is insurance. Insurance that this derelict won't go running to the cops. Insurance that he will continue to help me.

"You and I are going to make a deal," I say.

"Best news I've heard all day," he replies.

"I'm going to tell you who I truly am," I say, "because when you find out, I'll know for sure that you won't cross me."

"I already know who you are. You're Lucifer Raven, a drug lord from California."

"Right. You know that. But what you don't know is the extent of my power."

"Who says I don't?"

"Because if you did, you wouldn't be sitting here now."

His mouth drops open.

"Watch out for mosquitoes," I say.

He presses his lips together, his jaw rigid.

"You know my street name is Lucifer Raven, and you know I used to be involved in the drug business."

"Isn't that enough?"

"No, it's not, because if you truly knew who I was, you could've destroyed me."

"Oh?" His eyes widen.

"But you won't. Because now I know who *you* are, and I have connections that you can't even imagine."

He visibly shudders once more.

"I sit here, and I hold a gun on you. I could easily shoot you right now. I've done it before, you know. Just the fact that you ever harmed Katelyn is enough to make me want to blow your head off. I'm not going to. I'm not going to for one simple reason. I need you alive, for reasons I'm going to keep to myself for now. You need *me* alive, because without me, your protection goes out the window."

"You're offering me protection?"

"No, I'm offering you a deal, and here are the terms. I will protect you, see that no harm comes to you, and you'll do the same for me."

"Why would I want to do that?"

"Because if you don't, I'll have you sliced open."

He opens his mouth but then shuts it, clearly thinking better of arguing with me.

"You're right. My street name is Lucifer Raven. But my real name is...Lucifer Charles Ashton the third."

His eyebrows nearly fly off his forehead. "You're related to that producer?"

"Do you think a lot of people are named Lucifer?"

"I just assumed it was part of your street name. Your real name is Luke something."

"We're not all that different, Pollack. Except that I never

54

visited that island with my old man. I never did those horrible things that you did to women."

"Exactly how are we similar?" he says.

"Not in any way that I'm proud of. That's all I'll say. But here's what I *will* tell you. My connections go much farther than some simple drug lords. I know the people with the *real* power, both in the underground and in real life. My old man could have you offed in a second. So could the drug kingpins in LA. All it would take is a simple phone call from me. And... if anything happens to me? They have their orders."

His lips tremble. "What orders?"

"Three guesses, and the first two don't count."

He inhales. Exhales. A shudder racks through his body. "Fine. You have a deal."

"Good enough. Since you won't tell me what you did to Katelyn, I won't push it. You're going to give me something in return for not pushing it."

What I don't tell him is that I'm almost glad he won't tell me. If I truly knew? I'm not sure my newfound mental health would keep me from gutting him right here and now.

"All right." His gaze doesn't waver from my gun.

"You're not going to leave this place. In fact, I'm going to have someone watching you at all times."

"I have a job," he says.

"What the hell do you do?"

"I'm an—"

"Doesn't matter," I say. "You had enough money to go to that damned island. Even with the fine you paid, you can easily stay here and not go anywhere. You're at my fucking beck and call. Is that clear?"

"Who... Who will be watching me?"

"What fun would this be if I told you that? Just know that

I've got someone good on you at all times. You move? I'll know. Their orders are to kill."

"Oh... Okay." His voice cracks.

Good. He's scared.

No one will be watching, of course. What he doesn't know won't hurt him.

And now he knows who I really am.

That will be enough to keep him quiet. If my father was on that island and escaped incarceration, he can easily have Pollack killed without blinking an eye.

"I'm going to go now. You're going to lock yourself in. You will order your groceries to be delivered. That is that."

"I understand."

"Make the call."

"To whom?"

"To whoever you work with. Your boss. Tell him or her that you have a family emergency, and you have to take an unpaid leave of absence for an indefinite period of time."

"I can't just—"

"I wasn't asking."

"Fine. My phone... It's in my pocket."

"Well, get it out. You're acting like someone has a gun held to your head." I can't help a caustic laugh.

"I have your permission. To get my phone."

"You do. You're going to make the call, and you're going to put it on speaker. Because I don't really trust you not to call someone else and try to maneuver out of our deal."

"I wouldn't."

"Yeah, you probably wouldn't. You'd be stupid to try. Funny thing is...I still don't trust you."

Slowly, he reaches into his back pocket and pulls out a smart phone. He punches a number.

"Hi, Darlene. It's Chris. I need to talk to Ray."

"Sure, Chris. I'll patch you through."

Pause.

"Hey, Chris, what's up?"

"Sorry I didn't get in today. I've got a family emergency."

"Oh my. Anything I can do to help?"

"No, I can't really talk about it." Pollack's voice cracks, and he clears his throat. "I'm going to need to take an indefinite leave of absence. I don't expect to be paid."

"I can give you your PTO, and then yeah, it'll be unpaid."

"That's fine. Sorry for the inconvenience and for the short notice."

"No problem. We all have families. Let me know if we can do anything for you."

"Sure. I will." Another throat clear. "Thanks, Ray."

"No problem. Take care."

Pollack ends the call. "Satisfied?"

"Not even close. But at least I know where you are. My guys will be giving me hourly updates, so if you try to escape, you're going to have an issue."

He nods. "I understand."

"I'll be in touch." I rise finally, strap my gun back to my ankle and secure my knife. "Have a fucking nice day."

Once I'm out of his apartment I make a call.

It's not a call I ever wanted to make.

But I make it anyway.

"Yeah?" the familiar voice says.

"It's me, Dad."

12

KATELYN

I feel pretty good after coffee with Aspen. We're not besties or anything, but it was nice to talk.

Back at my place, my phone rings.

"Oh, crap," I say aloud. Then, into the phone, "Hi, Mom."

"Katelyn, darling, I just wanted to check in with you and see how you're doing."

"As well as to be expected, I'm sure. Is that really why you're calling?"

A pause. "That and I'd like you to come home."

"We've had this conversation, Mom. I'm better off here for now."

"I'm going to have to put my foot down. We need you home, Katelyn. You're my only child."

What would my mother think if she knew how I ended up on that island? How family members—family members she sent me to for the summer—turned me over to the priest?

"I didn't want to have to tell you this," she says, "but it's Dad. He..."

My heart jumps. "What? What's wrong with Dad?"

"I'm afraid he's sick, Katelyn. He has a tumor. On his liver."

"Is it malignant?"

"We don't know yet. He's going in for surgery to have a biopsy next week. I'd like you to come home."

"Mom, I just got a new job. I start on Monday."

"Is your new job more important than your father's health?"

"Of course not, but there's nothing I can do. You can let me know what the results are. I don't need to be there for the surgery. People are depending on me here."

"*I'm* depending on you, Katelyn. You're my only child. I need your support."

I roll my eyes.

I love my father. I love my mother too, but reclaiming my life is not conducive to being around her. "What are the chances that it's malignant?"

She pauses once more. Then, "It's most likely benign."

Classic Farrah Brooks.

Dad is the one facing a potential health crisis, which is most likely benign, but she's turned it into *everyone needs to support me*.

I'm not sure she even cares if my father's ill. Doesn't matter anyway. I have a new job, and I can't come home.

"Keep me in the loop," I tell her. "If it turns out the tumor is malignant, I'll see what I can do."

"Katelyn, how can you be so selfish?"

My jaw drops, though I'm not sure why. This behavior is on-brand for her. At least, it was before I disappeared. You'd think she might be a little more supportive of me, knowing what I've been through.

Clearly that's not going to happen.

Again, classic Farrah.

"This conversation is over, Mom. I can't do this right now."

"Katelyn, I'm sorry. It's just... I'm your mother. I need your support."

No, I will *not* let her get to me. I already went on a crying bender today over Luke. This woman cannot affect me this way.

I swallow. Give myself a few seconds to compose myself.

"I need *your* support, Mom. I was held for ten years against my will. Unspeakable things were done to my body. Unspeakable things were done to my mind. Did you know I have scars on my back from where I was whipped with a yardstick? Did you know I have scars from cuts all over my body? Did you know a man used to urinate on me? I've been raped, beaten, tortured. I think I need *your* support right now."

"Katelyn, I'm not trying to belittle what happened to you."

"No, you're not trying," I say. "Clearly it just comes naturally. Look, I hope Dad is okay. If it turns out that he's sick, I will come home. Right now, I have a job. A major company has trusted me with a high position, and I'm not about to let them down. I owe these people everything."

"Who do you owe everything?"

"The Wolfes."

"You owe your life to me and your dad," she says. "Without us, you wouldn't exist."

"You really want to play that card?" I shake my head, knowing full well she can't see me. "Sure, I owe you my life. Have you talked to Aunt Agnes lately?"

"Agnes? No."

"Don't you think it's interesting that I disappeared while I was on a visit to Aunt Agnes and Uncle Bruno?"

"You can't be blaming Agnes and Bruno."

"No. I'm not blaming Aunt Agnes and Uncle Bruno. I love them. Their sons did something that I cannot forgive."

"I don't know what you're talking about."

"Did any of the stuff I just said to you bother you at all? The fact that your only daughter was tortured and raped? Physically and emotionally abused?"

"Of course, Katelyn."

"Then understand that I need this. I need to be here. I need to complete my healing. I need to try to pay back the Wolfe family who has done so much for me."

"So this new family of yours trumps your old family?"

"Until Dad is terminal, yes, they do." I end the call.

How do I deal with the rage? How do I deal with the fact that I want to burst into sobs again? I can't let my mother get to me like this.

I just can't.

What can I do? The workout room. I quickly change into some sweats and head downstairs.

I was never a gym rat as a kid. And on the island, we were fed just enough to keep us thin and beautiful. The hunting gave us all the exercise we needed.

I slide my card through the door and walk into the gym. Exercise bikes, treadmills, ellipticals, weight machines. The steam room and sauna. Showers.

I don't know how to use any of this equipment, and no one is here to instruct me. I take a look at the treadmill first. Seems pretty easy. The digital display allows me to figure out exactly which settings I need.

But who the hell wants to walk on a machine? The bikes

and the ellipticals are much the same. User-friendly. And the weight machines.

This is not working. I don't want to work out. But I do need to do something to take the edge off. I look down at my running shoes. They're brand new and were in the closet when I got to the new apartment.

Run. I want to run.

I slide my key into my pocket along with my phone, I whisk past security, not bothering to tell the person on duty where I'm going, and leave the building.

And I run.

I whisk past the people walking down the busy city street, past the vendors, past the musicians playing for a few coins tossed into their guitar cases.

I run.

I run and I run and I—

Whomp!

I land on the sidewalk. On my ass.

Strong arms lift me. "Oh my God, I'm so sorry. Are you okay?" Blue eyes sear into mine.

"Yeah. Clearly I wasn't watching where I was going."

"It's totally my fault," the man says. "I'm late for a meeting at the Wolfe building."

"The Wolfe building?"

"Yeah, you know it?"

"I think everyone does. I work there. Or I'm going to be working there as of Monday."

"Really?" he says. "I'm interviewing for a position with Legal."

"You're a lawyer?

"Guilty. But please don't think less of me." He gives me a dazzling smile.

"You should be able to make it. Your almost there."

"Can I tempt you to have a cup of coffee with me after my interview?"

I freeze. "I...uh..."

He pulls a card out of his coat pocket. "If you change your mind, give me a call."

I bite my lower lip.

"I'd love to stay and talk to you, but I am going to be late. I'm so sorry about bumping into you."

"It's no problem."

"Good." He flashes me another smile. "I hope I hear from you." He waves and walks away briskly, looking over his shoulder and still smiling.

I drop my gaze to the card. Lance Stone.

What a name. Sounds like a porn star.

Lance Stone has beautiful blue eyes, close-cropped blond hair, and a nice smile. A very nice smile.

I don't feel so much as a tingle.

Not surprising, given what I've been through. However, there was no lack of a tingle when I first laid eyes on Luke.

I walk by a trashcan, ready to throw Lance's card in it, when something stops me.

Instead, I shove the card into my pocket.

13

LUKE

"What do you want, Trey?" my father demands.

Trey. For Lucifer the third. Everyone called me Trey when I was growing up. Everyone except my mother.

"Why the hell are you contacting me?" Dad demands again.

"I'm coming back. To LA."

"No, you're not. Do you know how much money I paid to get you out of the mess you're in? If you come back, King will see you dead."

"That's the chance I'm going to have to take."

"Are you kidding me? If anything happens to you, it will kill your mother."

His words are not lost on me. My mother—the woman who gave me life—never gave up on me, no matter what.

My father continues, "When you left home and got into the drug trade, it nearly killed her then. You were stabbed twice, Trey, and then shot."

"I was shot in the shoulder. My life was never in danger."

"Your life was in danger the moment you stepped into that world. I'm not sure you understand how much it took to get you out of it."

"Damn it, Dad, I do understand. And I'm grateful, but you know what? I just found out something about you that kind of makes my stomach turn."

"As much as finding out your son and namesake has left your world to deal drugs?"

"Yeah. What I did was illegal and disgusting. What you did...? It's worse."

"And what might this imaginary thing be?"

"Treasure Island."

No response.

Not that I expect one.

Finally, he clears his throat. "A book. By Robert Louis Stevenson."

"A private island," I counter. "Owned by Derek Wolfe."

Silence on the other end of the line once more.

"You went there, didn't you?"

"I don't know what you're talking about."

"Don't you?"

Silence for the third time.

"Look, you have lost the right to judge me," I say, clenching my teeth. "What I did was wrong on so many levels. I broke the law. I harmed people."

"You did more than that, Trey. You ordered some people killed."

"People the world is better off without."

"Some would say that about you."

His words are not lost on me. Sure, I got off alcohol. I

went through therapy, I'm changing my life for the better. None of that erases what I did in the past.

Which is why I'm going back to LA.

I clear my throat. "I never visited Treasure Island," I say in a robotic tone. "I never hunted women, tortured women, raped women."

"Some of your girlfriends might say differently."

Anger erupts in me. That snake-like rage that I work so hard to control. "I admit my mistakes, Dad. I let my rage get to me more than once with regard to women. But I never raped them. I never hunted them."

"So then there are degrees of evil? Is that what you're saying?"

What exactly *am* I saying? Are there degrees? Emily and a few others probably think I'm the devil himself. A testament to my name.

But Katelyn... The men who harmed her... The men like my father...

All of those women would probably say yes, there *are* degrees.

"Degrees aren't the point, Dad. The point is that you went to that island."

"Who says I went to that island?"

"A reliable source."

"More reliable than your own father?"

"You really want to go there, Dad? I'll take responsibility for my own actions. I'm not going to blame you or anyone else for the decisions I made. But take a good look in the mirror sometime. If your namesake had been happy, would he have made the decisions he made?"

"So I'm responsible for your happiness now?"

"You're not responsible for anything but your own

actions, just as I am. But take a look in the mirror," I say again. "And tell me if you like what you see. Tell me if there isn't a part of you that is responsible for what happened to your children."

"Your brother and your sister are fine."

I stop myself from letting out a guffaw. My brother and sister are far from fine. Not that I've talked to them anytime recently, but I do know they hold no love for our father.

"Maybe they are, and maybe they aren't. They're responsible for their own lives just as I'm responsible for mine. And just as you're responsible for yours. Tell me, Dad, how did you escape going to prison?"

Silence.

"It's a rhetorical question, after all. I know the answer. You pay people off."

"You didn't have a problem with me paying people off when it got you out of town."

"Maybe I did have a problem with it. I'm coming back. I'm coming back to LA."

"You're not. If you come back here, you and I both know what will happen. You will *not* do that to your mother."

I close my eyes. I don't want to harm my mother. But the fact that he's throwing her in my face really pisses me off. After what he's done to her over the years.

I give myself a few seconds to cool off. I must stay focused.

Finally, "I've got red on my ledger, Dad."

"Your ledger is nothing *but* red," he says. "You come back here, and you'll be killed within minutes."

"No, I won't be," I say. "Because you are going to help me."

"You think I have that kind of power?"

"I think," I say, "you don't want the entire world to know that you were on that island abusing women."

"You can't prove that."

"As a matter fact, I can."

Pollack may not be good for much, but he's at least good for that. Plus... Katelyn's going to be working for the Wolfes, and they must have information on all the men who visited that island.

"And I'm supposed to believe you because..."

"Because I know some of the men who were on that island, who played canary to stay out of prison.

Silence again, and this time for longer.

Good. I have his attention now.

"What the fuck do you want, Trey?"

"Your protection." I inhale, exhale slowly. "I'm coming home."

He sighs. "What do you need?"

"I've got my IDs. I was planning on taking a bus, but I got waylaid by someone who knew my street name. Apparently the bus isn't any more anonymous than an airplane or renting a car. I decided to fly. I'll take my chance using my fake IDs. I will be in LA by tomorrow."

"You didn't answer my question."

"I did. I need your protection. Make sure eyes are somewhere other than on me as I'm crossing the country. We've got FBI contacts. We've got money."

"You just told me yourself that someone found your street name," he says.

"Yes. Someone did. But that's all he found out. However, he now knows exactly who I am, and Dad? He's the one who told me you were on that island."

Slam and dunk.

"Who the fuck are you talking to?" Dad says.

"I'm going to keep that information to myself for now. In the meantime, I'll see you tomorrow."

I end the call.

I don't want to leave Katelyn. But she's better off without me.

Still... I can't go without seeing her one more time.

I press in her number.

14

KATELYN

My phone buzzes. It's Luke.

"Hello," I say without much emotion.

"It's me, baby. I need to see you."

"You know I can't let you into my place."

"I understand. Can you meet me at my place?"

"Luke...you almost left without me."

"I know, and I will not make that mistake again. Please, baby. Meet me. We need to talk."

I sigh. "All right. When?"

"As soon as possible."

I'm heading back to my place after finishing my run. I'm dripping with perspiration and wearing sweats. "I need a shower."

"You can shower here."

"I showered there this morning."

Is it really the same day? I feel like weeks have passed.

"I'll shower at my place, Luke. Then I'll come over. Are you working tonight?"

"I'm not, Katelyn. Please, come quickly."

"All right."

"I love you."

"I love you too." I shove my phone back in my pocket and head to the building.

I shower, blow dry my hair, and then dress in jeans and a simple camisole. I want to look good for Luke, but I also don't want to. I can't get my hopes up.

Something's up. I can tell in his voice.

I throw my sweats into the hamper but then remember something. I pull out Lance Stone's card.

I hold it, looking at his name and his phone number. It's not a business card. It's a simple calling card—the kind rich people carry around with them.

Is Lance Stone rich? He's an attorney, obviously, if he's applying to the legal department at Wolfe Enterprises.

Maybe he comes from money.

Stone. The name doesn't sound familiar, but I hardly know the names of all the rich people in New York. I've crossed paths with a lot of them, but they were all Mr. Smiths and Mr. Joneses. No one gave a real name on the island.

I bite my lip. Why am I having a hard time throwing the card away? Doesn't make any sense. I'm in love with Luke. As attractive as Lance Stone was, I didn't feel a tingle.

Throw it away, Katelyn.

But I don't. I open my top dresser drawer and slide the card under my underwear.

Then I go downstairs and hail a cab to take me to Luke's.

LUKE OPENS the door for me. "Hey, baby."

"Hi."

"You look beautiful."

"Thank you."

Luke looks devastating, of course. He's wearing jeans and a black button-down. His eyes are as dark and memorizing as ever.

Except they're not his eyes. Chills hit me like a gust of wind.

The colored contacts.

"Luke?"

"Yeah, baby?"

"What color are your eyes?"

"They're brown."

"Are they? Truly?"

"Why are you asking me this, Katelyn?"

"You're forgetting that you left me here this morning. You also left something in your mirrored cabinet above the sink."

He drops his gaze to the floor.

"I saw the contacts, Luke. The colored contacts."

"Katelyn, I—"

"You were going to leave me early this morning. Without saying goodbye. But there's a lot of other stuff you're not saying too, isn't there?"

"Baby..."

I inhale. I must stay strong. Although even now, I'm getting the tingles that I always get in Luke's presence.

"Please don't," I say. "Please... No more lies."

"Katelyn—"

"No. No. Just... No."

My mind is blurred. Words fly around inside my head, but I can't make any cogent sense of them. What color are Luke's eyes? Maybe they *are* brown. Maybe there's a reason he wears the brown contacts. I don't know anything about optometry or ophthalmology. There could be a good reason, right?

Except I already know I'm grasping at straws.

"Katelyn," Luke says, "are you all right?"

No, I'm not all right. But I don't say the words. I can't make them come out of my throat. I'm in a daze. A daze or haze or just a mess. Am I concussing? Having a stroke?

Something is going on in my mind and I—

I gasp as my legs crumple beneath me, and I fall to the floor.

15

LUKE

"Baby!" I lift her into my arms. "Fuck, what have I done to you?"

My heart beats rapidly. *Katelyn, my Katelyn.* I place her on my bed, which is still unmade from when she was here this morning.

"What have I done?" I say again.

A soft sigh escapes her lips, and her eyes open slowly.

"Katelyn?"

She doesn't speak. I brush my lips over her softly. "I'm so sorry."

"Are your eyes really brown?" she whispers.

I know better. I know better than to tell her anything about my disguise.

I have to get to LA safely. If I don't, I won't be able to right the wrongs.

I hold back a scoff. It would take three lifetimes to right all of my wrongs. I knew this going in.

Is it even worth trying?

I have to now. I told Pollack who I was, and I called my father.

I already have my flight booked to LA tomorrow morning. I don't have a choice.

And I know I can't be what Katelyn needs unless I fix as much as I can.

It's a done deal.

"I'll be right back, baby." I push her hair off her forehead.

I rise slowly, so as not to nudge her. I want to keep her comfortable. Then I go to the bathroom, and I remove my colored contact lenses. My vision is perfect. I've never needed correction, so these contact lenses are for nothing more than cosmetic purposes.

To change my stark blue eyes to brown.

My naturally blond hair is covered by the hair dye. Nothing can be done about that. It will have to grow out. For now it stays short and brown.

As I stare at myself in the mirror, my actual reflection stares back at me, as if the mirror only shows what I truly am.

Long blond hair. Blue eyes. Scruffy blond stubble.

I've remained closely shaven since I started this charade. Sandy blond stubble wouldn't really jibe with the dark brown hair.

The shirt I'm wearing seems to dissolve in front of my eyes, showing more accuracy in my reflection. My bare chest —no dark hair, since I'm not dark-haired. The scar from my stab wound to the stomach, and then my most recent scar— the bullet to my shoulder.

And, of course, the tattoo that begins on my left hand and winds all the way up my left arm to my shoulder.

The Raven with flaming wings.

Lucifer Raven.

My dark side.

Funny. I'm a blond and blue-eyed man, but the name Raven stuck.

I remember when I got it.

~

"TELL ME SOMETHING, RICH BOY," King says.

King is actually his real name. Short for Kingsford Winston. His goons jumped me when I was walking around a seedy part of LA. A place where I had no business being, but I was a rebel in those days.

I was rebelling against my old man.

Even against my mother.

I was twenty-one and rebelling against anything.

But unlike James Dean, I was not a rebel without a cause. My old man threatened to cut me off if I didn't get my shit together.

Since I didn't give a rat's ass about him, I told him to go for it.

But not before pocketing as much cash as I could and getting it into my own name.

Still...I needed to make a living. I needed to find some way to make money.

Which is how I got involved with King.

"You think you're worthy?" he asks me.

"I can handle a gun like nobody's business," I say. "And I'm a third-degree black belt in judo."

"How'd that happen, rich boy?"

"How do you think? My old man paid for all of it. I had the best lessons money could buy."

"And how am I supposed to trust that you aren't going to go running back to that world?"

"That world turned its back on me."

"*I hear you, rich boy. The world turned its back on me a long time ago.*"

Interesting. Seems I have something in common with this drug lord.

"*This is not an easy life, rich boy,*" *he says.*

"*I'm not looking for easy.*"

"*What* are *you looking for?*"

"*I want to make more money than my old man can ever dream of.*"

"*Your old man's a multimillionaire. Close to a billion, I hear. Drugs aren't a billion-dollar industry, at least not for any one person. But...you* can *make in the hundreds of millions if you play your cards right.*"

"*How do I play my cards right?*" *I ask.*

"*First, you become indispensable to me.*"

"*Okay. Tell me what to do and I'll do it.*"

"*That's the thing. Everybody in the business wants to become indispensable to me. Only a few have made it. I don't give lessons, rich boy.*"

"*I guarantee I'll become indispensable to you,*" *I say,* "*but first you have to stop calling me rich boy.*"

"*I'll call you what I damned well please,*" *he says.*

Quick as a flash, I've got him on his back. Knife hand to his throat. "*Still going to call me rich boy?*"

"*No,*" *he says.* "*I like your first name, though. It's...satanic. Literally.*"

"*Thank my old man for that.*"

"*You're no longer an Ashton, and you're no longer rich boy. From now on, you're Raven. Lucifer Raven.*"

For some reason, the name seems to fit. Though I don't know why. "*Why Raven?*"

"*The Raven is intelligent and cunning. Already I can see those qualities in you, but the biggest one is survival and adaptability.*"

"*Are you some kind of shaman or something?*" I say sardonically.

"*Just a guy who knows a few things. Just a guy who puts a little faith in symbolism.*"

"*And you think I'm a survivor?*"

"I know *you are, Raven. You wouldn't be here otherwise.*"

16

KATELYN

I'm floating. Living on a comfy cloud.

I inhale, and Luke's scent infuses me—all spicy, wild man.

I open my eyes, and I remember. I'm here, Luke's place. He asked me to come, and I asked him about his eyes.

He walks toward me then and sits down on the bed.

"Katelyn," he says, "are you okay?"

"I think so. You look—" I gasp.

"You asked me about my eyes. They're blue, Katelyn. Not nearly as beautiful as your blue eyes, but they're blue."

"Why?" I ask.

"I have my reasons. I'll tell you all of them, but not right now. Right now I just want to be with you."

"Luke, I—"

He covers my lips with his fingers, just a gentle nudge to get me to quit speaking.

"Please, baby, let me love you. I need you so badly."

My nipples harden, and the tingles... The tingles that are always present when Luke is near surge through me. Why would he keep those gorgeous blue eyes a secret? And the hair. There must be a story there.

I open my mouth, but he kisses me. Kisses me hard with his tongue and lips and teeth.

I shouldn't let him off the hook so easily, but I can't help myself. I love him. I love this man—this man who kept things from me.

Can this work? I don't know because my only experience with men during the last ten years was on the island. Men who were masquerading. Wearing fake names as masks—sometimes wearing actual masks—to lie, to abuse, to torture.

I don't like lies.

I should break this kiss. I should demand an explanation.

Yet I can't stop kissing him. The force between us—the chemistry, the sheer magnetism we seem to share—I can't control it. I can't stop it.

What's more? I don't want to stop it.

He deepens the kiss, taking my tongue with his, exploring my mouth with his warmth and his passion.

I give in.

It's so easy to give in.

Again I revel in the fact that I never thought I'd feel this way. I never thought I would want to be so close to any man.

With Luke, things are so different.

So what if his eyes aren't brown? They're a lovely blue—darker than my own and more intense.

I open my eyes, hoping to get a glimpse of them. But his eyes are closed.

He moves on top of me, keeping his weight on his upper arms so he doesn't crush me, but grinding into me. He's hard—so hard—and he pushes the bulge in his jeans against my clit.

My body is on fire. So hot, and I want him so badly.

He was going to leave me.

He was going to—

I push him away, and the kiss breaks with a loud smack.

"Baby?" he says.

"I can't, Luke. I can't do this. Why are you hiding the beautiful color of your eyes? Why were you going to leave me? And what brought you back?"

"Katelyn, I... It's a long story, and I don't... No, I can't... I can't get into it right now."

"I can't either, then," I say. "I need something real in my life, Luke. Something real and solid and wonderful. I thought it was you. But now I'm not so sure."

"Are you saying your feelings for me have changed?"

"God, no. They haven't changed. How do you fall *out* of love? Just because I find out the man I'm in love with lied to me about the color of his eyes doesn't mean I fell out of love."

"I didn't lie to you."

"You covered them up. Isn't that the same thing?"

"Maybe I had a reason for doing that."

"Why? Tell me the reason, then."

"It wasn't to lie to you. That I can promise you."

"Then it was to lie to someone else?"

"It's more complicated than that, Katelyn. I'm kind of...in hiding."

My stomach cramps up. "Hiding from whom?"

"From a lot of people. If I tell you... Never mind. I just can't tell you."

"Why can't you? Maybe I can help."

"You can't. The only person who can help me is *me*."

"Does this have anything to do with why you left me in the middle of the night?"

"I'm afraid it does. Katelyn, I love you. I never imagined loving anyone the way I love you."

His words warm me. They warm me because I feel them too. I open my mouth to return the sentiment, but he keeps talking.

"I want to be Luke Johnson more than anything."

"You *are* Luke Johnson."

"But I'm not. Not really. I tried to blend in. I tried to be every man. The kind of guy no one would notice."

"You're never going to be the kind of guy no one notices, Luke."

"You're right about that," he says, "but not for the reason you think."

"You can trust me. I'll never harm you."

"I know you won't, baby. There isn't a vindictive bone in your body. But the less you know about me—about who I really am—the safer you'll be."

I shudder. My safety is at issue?

I lived the last ten years with my safety at issue at all times. Diamond always told us that our safety was a top priority. Sure, these men could violate us in whatever twisted ways they wanted, but they couldn't kill us.

So in that way, we were safe.

That was an interesting definition of the word safe.

But one thing's for sure. Not much scares me—I mean *truly* scares me—now.

"I'm not afraid," I say to Luke. "I've seen the worst in humanity. There's no way you're bad for me."

He rubs his forehead. "So much you don't know. *I'm* afraid. I'm afraid *for* you."

"Do you have any idea what I've been through? You saw the scars on my back. And I can tell you that a lot of things didn't leave scars—not physical ones anyway. Do you really think there's much that scares me in this world?"

"I don't know, Katelyn. But there is one thing that scares me."

"What's that?"

"Harm coming to you. I will do *anything* to keep you safe. And that means...keeping you out of my world."

"I don't accept that. I don't accept that at all. You're nothing like them. You can't get rid of me that easily."

He rakes his fingers through his short hair. "I don't want to get rid of you. I want to be with you. All I want is you, Katelyn. But I can't have you. Don't you see?"

"No, I don't see. I don't see at all. What I see is a man hiding from something. You hid your beautiful blue eyes from the world. What else are you hiding? I saw your hair dye in the bathroom. You don't really have that dark brown hair, do you?"

"I'm blond. Kind of a sandy blond."

"So why?"

"I can't," he says. "I can't."

"What *can* you do?" I ask.

"This." His lips come down on mine once more.

17

LUKE

I can't think about this. Can't think about any of this.

Just need to have Katelyn one more time.

If she breaks the kiss again, I don't know what I'll do. What if I can't have her one more time? What if I go to LA, lose my life, and never taste Katelyn's sweetness again?

She doesn't stop me, thank God. And as I kiss her I brush one strap of her camisole over her milky shoulder. I rip my lips from hers and kiss her neck, the top of her chest, her shoulder. My God, she's so beautiful, her skin like fresh cream. The texture is smooth under my lips, under my fingertips, and she tastes... She tastes like flesh and caramel.

I'm going to fuck her. It's not going to be nice and it's not going to be pretty. But I need her.

I roll off her and undress her quickly.

"Luke, you're going to rip the fabric."

"I don't care. I'll buy you a new one."

"On your waiter's salary? Luke, come on."

"I have money, baby. I have lots and lots of money. I'll buy you whatever you need."

And I will. First thing I'll do when I get to LA is call my lawyer and make sure Katelyn is well taken care of no matter what happens to me.

I manage to get the camisole off her without tearing the fine fabric. Her breasts... She's not wearing a bra, and oh my God, she's so beautiful.

I caress the round globes, skim over the hard nipples. She undulates beneath me, raising her hips, looking for something...

Something I'm ready to give her.

I'm so freaking hard. My dick is pulsing against my jeans. I need to free it, let it breathe, let it find what it's looking for—Katelyn's pussy.

"Feels good, Luke," she says on a soft breath.

"I'm going to suck on your nipples, Katelyn. Suck them and bite them and make you so crazy that you beg me to stop."

"I will never beg you to stop."

I believe her, but I go to work on a nipple anyway, first sucking it gently between my lips, relishing in her moans and undulations. Then I nibble it, taking it between my teeth, nipping it harder and harder and harder until I bite it.

"Oh!" she gasps.

But she doesn't tell me to stop.

I bite the nipple again while I pinch the other one between my fingers.

But then I stop. I let the nipple drop from my lips.

"What?" she says.

I don't answer.

I picture Pollack or any of those other derelicts doing terrible things to Katelyn's body. Rage...that familiar fucking rage...

Her body should be treated like a shrine. Who am I to deface it?"

"Luke?"

"I'm sorry, baby. I love you, but..."

"What?"

"Those men... What they did to you... I'm so sorry. I shouldn't be touching you like this."

"Yes, you should. I want it."

"Even after I lied to you?"

She smiles weakly. "I suppose covering your true eye color wasn't exactly a lie."

"But I told you. I'm not Luke Johnson. My whole identity is a façade."

"And I thought that mattered," she says, cupping my cheek. "You know what? It doesn't. In a way, I'm a façade too. I'm not the same person I was before the island. I may never be the same person again."

"You are anything but a façade, Katelyn. You're one of the most real people I've ever met, and that's one of the reasons I love you so much. You could never be a façade."

"Tell me, then. Tell me what's real about you."

I sigh. "My eyes are blue and my hair is blond."

"You already told me that. Tell me something about the real you. The Luke that's inside."

"I am a recovering alcoholic," I say. "That's not a lie."

"Okay, that's a start. What else?"

"My alcoholism... It made me..."

"It made you what?"

"It made me *mean*, Katelyn. It made me do things that I shouldn't have done. But that's not even the whole story. I was different then. I can't blame it all on the alcohol. Sure, the alcohol pushed me over the edge, but it was *me*. I'm the one who did those things, and I have to own them."

She strokes my cheeks, gazes at me with such love and wonder in her beautiful eyes.

"What things did you do, Luke? Nothing can be that bad."

Nothing can be that bad.

Except what I did was worse than that. I harmed people. I got people hooked on drugs. I tried to control women, and in doing so I hurt them. And I had people…

I had people taken care of.

Such a stupid-ass euphemism.

I had people killed. Sure, they were bad guys, but to them? I was the bad guy.

How do I erase that red off my ledger?

By saving a life for each one I helped to take?

God… I haven't let myself think about this in so long. I had therapy. Therapy helped. Helped me realize I was worth something, worthy of a second chance.

But am I? Truly?

What if I can never make up for the horrible things I've done?

The devil on my shoulder taunts me. *You're worse than the devil you were named for. You'll never be a whole man. You'll never be good enough for Katelyn.*

The angel in my other shoulder— *The people who are no longer in the world because of you were bad people. They would've harmed others, and you saved others from that harm.*

I don't believe either one.

All I know—just this one thing—is that I love this woman. I love Katelyn Brooks. And I'm going to make love to her one more time.

"You're not mean to me," Katelyn says. "Except for…"

"Except I left you. Or I tried to."

If not for Pollack, I'd be on that damned bus right now.

Am I truly thankful for Pollack's intervention?

Damn, maybe I am.

This way, Katelyn at least knows I'm leaving. She may not understand—I don't even want her to understand—but at least she knows.

"You did," she says. "But you know what? It doesn't even matter, Luke. I forgive you. I forgive you for hiding your eye color, your hair color. I forgive you for trying to escape in the middle of the night and leave me. I forgive you for everything, and I will always forgive you for everything because I love you. I love you so much. You don't know how much that means to me. I didn't think I'd ever love. Not after what I've been through. You... You made me see that it's possible to love. And even if you leave me tomorrow and I never see you again, I will always be grateful to you for that."

I groan. And it's a groan not just of horniness and sexual desire but of amazement. Amazement that a woman like Katelyn exists in this world. A woman who can forgive me anything.

Would she truly forgive me anything if she knew everything I'd done?

She thinks she can, and whether or not it's true, at least I know she loves me now.

She wants me now.

Just as I love her and want her.

"I need to make love to you, Katelyn," I say. "Please."

"I never stopped you in the first place."

I smile weakly. "No, you didn't. Thank you. Thank you for just... For being you. For being so perfect and loving and forgiving."

"I do love you, Luke."

"And I love you, my beautiful, sweet Katelyn." I kiss her.

I kiss her with all the pent-up energy and passion I have in me. Her shirt is gone, her chest beckons, and I trail kisses over her cheeks, her neck, shoulders, the tops of her breasts.

She moans as I take her nipples between my lips, suck them, bite them, lick them.

With one hand, I work the buttons on her pants. Then I slide my hand inside, find her hard clit, and rub her.

She gasps, undulating her hips, and I know I found the right spot.

"Please..." she moans.

I roll off her, shed my clothing in record time. Then I take care of her shoes, pants, and underwear. Her clothes are in a pile on the floor, and we're naked. Together on my bed.

How I want to take my time, love her as she deserves to be loved.

But my cock has other ideas. She's already wet. Her slick juices coat my fingers.

She's wet and ready, and I mount her and thrust into her.

"God, Katelyn," I groan.

I feel every ridge inside her, every succulent crease of her pussy. I pull out and thrust back in. Again. Again. Again.

I won't last long at this rate, but I want her to have an orgasm.

I pull out.

God, the loss! I'm empty. And the emptiness... I know it will never go away once I leave her.

She deserves more than a quick fuck. This may be our last time.

I spread her legs, regard the beauty between them. She's pink and swollen, glistening with her own cream.

I slide my tongue through her folds, savor the sweetness.

She shudders beneath me. "Luke, I want you inside me."

"Soon," I say, determined not to be selfish and take my own pleasure before she has hers.

"But please," she begs.

"You're not making this easy, baby. I want to take care of you first. Please. Let me do this for you."

She relents, sighing.

"I'm going to eat you. I'm going to lick you and suck you until you can't take it anymore." I close my lips around her clit and suck gently.

She grabs the comforter, groans, arching her back.

I move from her clit and shove my tongue into her wetness. She tastes like a dream. I could eat her forever. Although my cock is so hard, it's sheer torture not to just fuck her.

But eat her I will. And I will take pleasure in it because she tastes like perfection, and I love her more than anything.

I swipe my tongue over her clit once more, and then I push her thighs forward. Her sweet puckered asshole beckons, but...she's not ready for that.

Sadness whips through me as I realize I will probably never be able to take her there.

I'll be dead before—

No. Not going there.

Even the thought of death, though, hasn't stopped my cock from throbbing. Katelyn has that big of an effect on me.

I continue my assault on her pussy—licking, sucking, eating.

She groans above me, murmurs my name, raises her hips, slides against my face in tandem with my tongue-lashing. And then—

"Luke!"

Her flesh vibrates against my mouth as she climaxes. I shove a finger inside her, find her G-spot, to make her orgasm last even longer.

Her moans continue, and my cock grows harder. Harder. Harder.

I want to make her come again. Again and again and again, but my cock...

I need her so badly. I need to be inside her.

While she's still in the middle of her climax, I crawl atop her and plunge in.

God, yes. Her pussy quivers around my cock, milking me.

I know I won't be long, but I pull out and thrust and again. Again. Again. Again.

My release sneaks up on me quickly. Even quicker than I expect. My balls scrunch up to my body, and every contraction shatters me as I empty myself into her.

And I wonder...

Will I ever feel as complete as I do now?

18

KATELYN

The ultimate hug. Making love is the ultimate hug.

The thought surprises me—in the midst of a climax, no less.

This is the closest I can be to another person, yet...

Yet...

I want more.

I want more of Luke. How do I get even more?

He stays inside me once both of our climaxes come to a rest.

He still doesn't leave me when he rolls to his side, taking me with him. We lie face-to-face, still joined by our bodies.

I don't ever want to leave this place.

I open my eyes. He's looking at me. His eyes are so blue. Like the ocean at dusk.

"I don't know why you hid these beautiful eyes," I say.

He doesn't reply.

He must have a reason, but in my post-orgasmic haze, I don't really care.

All I know is that I love him. I need him.

"You're staying now, right?"

Again, he doesn't reply.

I should be sad. And I will be, once the haze of my orgasm dissipates.

For now, I'm floating on a cloud with Luke, his dick still embedded inside me, my walls still clasping him.

I close my eyes and sigh.

And I wish I could stay here forever.

Too soon, though, Luke moves away from me, and his cock slides out of me. I whimper at the loss, but I knew this wouldn't last forever.

"Katelyn..."

The tone of his voice is...so *sad*.

"Yes?"

"I'm leaving."

And just like that, my post-orgasmic bliss is gone.

"No," I say. "You absolutely can't leave me."

"I have to. I'm not..."

"What? You're not what?"

"I just... There's some stuff I need to work out."

"What kind of stuff?"

He doesn't reply for a moment, and just when I think he's going to give me the silent treatment once more, he finally speaks.

"I'm not a good man, Katelyn."

"You're the *best* man."

"I want to be."

"Then you *are*, Luke."

"If only it were that simple."

"But don't you see? It *is* that simple. As a man thinketh."

"What?"

"*As a Man Thinketh*. It's a book. My—" I stop.

I was about to say my Aunt Agnes gave me the book. When I was fourteen. The last summer I spent at the brownstone in Brooklyn...until I was eighteen.

And then...

Funny. After everything I've been through, I haven't given the book a thought. But now, with Luke going through stuff of his own, it comes to mind.

Why didn't I think about it to help myself all those years?

And it dawns on me...

Sometimes it takes loving another to become what you're meant to be.

"Why did you stop, Katelyn? Tell me about this book."

"It's not a book so much as an essay. You know, a really short book. Who was the author? A guy named James Allen, I think. Anyway, the message is pretty universal. Basically, you are what you think you are."

"I see."

"So as long as you think you're not worthy, you aren't. But I can tell you that you are. You're worthy of everything."

"Katelyn, *you* are worthy of everything."

"You know what? You're right. I know that now. I kept my strength during those years. It was hard, but I didn't always have that strength, Luke. There was a time..." I inhale.

He raises his eyebrows, telling me to continue.

I blow out my breath slowly. "There was a time when I wanted to end my life."

He pulls me close to him, kisses the side of my neck. "Baby, no."

"You can't imagine what it was like for me."

"I can't. I absolutely can't. I don't think anyone can who hasn't lived it."

"Just imagine how bad you think it was, and then realize it was probably worse."

He pulls away then, meets my gaze. "I can't. I can't think of you like that, Katelyn. It will kill me. And I'll need to…"

"What?"

He curls his hands into fists. "Nothing. Never mind."

"It's okay. I love you. I got through the horror of those years. And whatever you're hiding, Luke, you've gotten through it. It's over."

"That's the problem, Katelyn. It's not over for me. It absolutely is *not* over."

19

LUKE

I rise then.

In a few moments, I'm dressed. I pick up Katelyn's clothes and set them on the bed for her. "I shouldn't have left you here last night," I say. "Your safety is the most important thing to me, and once I'm back in LA—"

"You're going back to LA?"

Damn. Probably shouldn't have said that. Something about Katelyn makes me want to be totally honest. However, if I *am* totally honest, she will go screaming and running away.

She can think she won't. She can think that our love is all that matters. In an ideal world, she's right.

We don't live in an ideal world.

But I can't lie to her. I'm keeping so much away from her as it is.

"Yes, I'm going back to LA."

"Why? What's going on?"

"Some things I need to take care of, baby. Family stuff."

She nods. "Actually...I have some family stuff in LA right now too. My dad is going in for a liver biopsy."

"I'm sorry. Is he okay?"

"Most likely. Chances are the tumor is benign, according to my mom. Of course she wants me to drop everything and go back there to support her. But I'm starting a new job on Monday. I told her I can't."

Thank God for Katelyn's new job. Otherwise, she would have a perfect excuse to go running back to LA with me.

I can't have that.

I can't have her anywhere near danger.

"I'm glad he's okay."

"Well, like I said, he's most likely okay."

"I'm also really happy for you about the job, Katelyn. I know you'll kill it."

"I hope so. Part of me wishes I could go back to LA. I don't want you to leave, Luke."

"I'll be back as soon as I can."

No lie there. I *will* be back as soon as I can. However, "as soon as I can" may be a long time, and I may not live through it.

I can't tell her that. I absolutely can't.

"Tell me about this job. What will you be doing?"

"I wish I knew. I'm totally not qualified for it, but Reid and Zee want to give me this chance. I hope I don't let them down."

"Baby, you could never let anyone down."

"Luke, I have no experience. I was a lifeguard when I was a teen. Then, on my way to college, I got taken. I have absolutely no work experience and certainly nothing that would help me in an office setting."

"But you're smart, you're strong, and you're willing to learn. That's probably what they see in you."

"Yeah. That's what they say, anyway."

"These people want to help you. All you have to do is let them."

"They feel responsible for me."

"While they're not personally responsible, Derek Wolfe is. They're trying to make up for what he did. I totally understand where they're coming from."

More than she knows. The problem? I'll never be able to totally make up for everything I've done. But I will try. And I will most likely die trying.

Perhaps the red will never be completely off my ledger, but I have to do something.

You've done something, the angel on my shoulder says. *You gave evidence to the authorities.*

That just makes you a canary, the devil on my other shoulder says.

They're both right. I still feel like shit.

"Yeah, I get how they're feeling," she says.

"Don't you worry. You're going to be fantastic."

"What will I do? You're not going to be here."

"Baby, I won't be of any help to you with your job."

"But just knowing that you're here. That will help me more than anything."

"I *will* be here," I say, touching her chest. "Right in here."

I get a smile out of her then. It's a weak smile, but at least it's a smile.

"I'll always be in your heart too, Luke."

"You will," I say.

"I just wish..."

"Me too, baby. Me too."

More than you know.

THE NEXT MORNING, I rise early. I sit next to Katelyn when I'm dressed.

"Wake up, baby. Time to go."

"You mean I can't stay here?"

"Not this time."

I left her here the last time, when my plan was to get on a bus to LA. But Pollack figured out who I was. Granted, all he found was my street name. He didn't know my true identity, and he also didn't know exactly what my street name meant, but he knew enough.

If a stupid ass like Pollack could figure that much out, who knows what someone with actual brainpower can, which means Katelyn is not safe at my place.

"I had to sublet this place." The lie is bitter on my tongue. I don't like lying to Katelyn. But this is for her own safety. "The new tenants will arrive later today."

"Sublet? You're going to be gone that long?"

"Probably for at least a month."

"I'll come visit you as soon as I can," she says.

"I'd love that."

It can't happen, of course. But again, I don't want to hurt her.

"So you'll call me?"

"As soon as I can," I say.

That isn't even a lie. The only issue is that I won't be able to for a while.

"All right." She gathers her clothes and dresses.

We didn't make love again last night, just held each other.

It seemed like the right thing to do.

I can't have her worried. I can't have her scared. I need her to be Katelyn. I need her to be whole for her new job. She needs it as much as I do.

"I'm going to get you a cab to take you back to your place." I sigh.

"Can't you take me? Walk with me?"

"I wish I could, but I have to get to the airport."

She nods. Not smiling.

"Hey," I say. "I love you, Katelyn. I will always, always love you."

"I love you too, Luke. Always and forever."

Once Katelyn is dressed, I walk her downstairs and hold the cab door for her. I kiss her lightly on the lips. I don't want to draw attention to us.

"Don't forget," I say, "I will always love you."

She nods, gets in the cab, and I close the door for her.

As the yellow sedan drives off, I stand.

I stand there long after the cab has disappeared from my sight.

And I wonder... Is it possible to feel your heart physically break?

Because I'm almost sure mine has cracked in two.

20

KATELYN

Monday morning, I attempt to throw myself into my work.

Luke hasn't called.

Not even to tell me he got to LA safely.

I texted the number that I have for him a couple of times, just to check in. One time, I saw the three dots move. My heart sped up as I waited for his response.

It never came.

Despite two more texts to him, I haven't heard a word.

As soon as I can.

His words reverberate throughout my mind.

I can believe one of two things. One, he no longer loves me and doesn't care. In my heart, I know that's not true. So it must be two—it's not yet possible for him to contact me.

The second thought frightens me, sends chills through my body.

During the last two days, I've come close to picking up the phone and purchasing a plane ticket to LA. My mother would be thrilled.

But I haven't done it. The Wolfes are depending on me for this job, which they gave me even though I'm completely not qualified.

I can't let them down. I owe them my life.

But in a way, I also owe Luke my life. Life isn't just existing. It's living.

Luke gave me something I thought might have been lost forever. He helped me reclaim my body. He helped me reclaim my heart and my soul.

I owe him as much as I do the Wolfes.

If only I knew what to do.

Zee is still on maternity leave. Can I even talk to her about this? She's loyal to the Wolfe family. She's *part* of the Wolfe family. Would she truly understand if my loyalty were split?

How could she?

I actually have an office. Surprised the heck out of me. It even has a small window. It's far from the corner office of an executive, but it's an office with a window. It's right next to Reid's corner office, and Alicia has an office next to me.

A personal assistant and a personal secretary who have their own offices.

This is pretty cushy, and I don't deserve it.

Alicia is standing over me, showing me how to work my computer. "Your schedule is here." She taps a key. "And here's Mr. Wolfe's schedule."

"We call him Mr. Wolfe here?"

"We do. Although in more social settings I call him Reid."

"Good to know."

"You get used to it. Apparently Mr. Wolfe Senior—"

I cringe.

"I'm sorry. I shouldn't have mentioned his name."

"No, it's okay. Despite what he did to me and others, he is the person who built this company."

"True. And apparently, he liked things to remain formal at the office. Once he died, things changed a bit, but we still call the Wolfes Mr. and Ms. over here."

"So I need to call Zee Ms. Wolfe when she comes in the office?"

"She'll probably make an exception for you. She considers you a friend."

"I consider her a friend as well. My best friend right now."

"I understand."

But does she? Probably not. It's not hurtful. I certainly don't wish anything bad on Alicia. She's a big reason why I have this job. Reid offered it to her first.

"Lunch is from noon to one," she says, "but nobody punches a timeclock here. You're on your own and on your honor. No one will care if you have to leave early one day. We just all have the expectation that the work will get done, and it does."

"I'm sure I'll be burning the midnight oil the next first couple weeks," I say, "since I don't have a clue what I'm doing."

"Don't sell yourself short," Alicia says. "You're going to do just fine."

I give her a weak smile. "I appreciate your confidence in me."

"I understand where you're coming from," she says. "The Wolfes do feel responsible for you, but they also have an incredible work ethic. If Reid didn't think you could handle this, he wouldn't have given you the job."

"Not even to appease his wife?"

She smiles. "Not even then."

Alicia has no reason to lie to me. After all, she could've had this job but chose not to take it.

"I will do my best," I affirm with as much strength as I can muster in my voice.

"Do you have any questions?"

"No. I think I'd like to just get to work."

"Well, the first thing you need to do is go down to HR. They're going to give you an orientation tour of the entire office."

"Isn't there something a little more important for me to do?"

"There are a ton of more important things for you to do," she says. "But all new employees have an orientation tour on the first day. It's standard around here."

I stand. "Okay. Lead the way."

Alicia walks me to the elevator. "Go down to the sixth floor. They're expecting you."

"Got it."

I get on the elevator and press six. Within a microsecond, the doors open on floor six. Right into the human resources department. I check in with reception.

"The HR manager will be out in a moment," the receptionist says. "Go ahead and have a seat."

I turn. A handsome young man sits in one of the chairs.

He stands when he sees me. "Hey, how are you?"

It's Lance Stone. The man I met the other day who was on his way to an appointment with legal department at Wolfe Enterprises.

"Good morning," I say. "I guess this means you got the job."

"I did. I'm really excited to be working with Ms. Wolfe and her staff."

"Ms. Wolfe?"

"Yeah, Lacey Wolfe. She's Rock's wife, head of Legal."

"Right." I knew that, of course. My mind is just...not where it should be on the first day of work.

That needs to stop now.

"I guess we'll be on the same orientation tour," he says. "I can't think of a greater companion."

His smile is sincere. Sincere and rather breathtaking.

Still... No tingles at all.

"You want some coffee?" Lance asks, nodding to the beverage station.

"No, thank you." I've already had two cups, and my heart is beating like a hummingbird's. No more caffeine for me, thank you very much. Besides, I don't want to have to excuse myself to hit the bathroom during some integral part of the tour.

"Good enough." He nods to another chair. "Have a seat."

I sit, but no sooner does my butt hit the plush leather when another young man whisks into the room.

"Morning," he says jovially. "You must be Katelyn and Lance. I'm Morgan Phillips, Jenny's assistant. She's on a conference call, so I'll be doing your orientation."

I remember Jenny from the paperwork I filled out when Reid first offered me the job. She's a middle-aged woman with a friendly smile.

Morgan is no less friendly, though he's bespectacled and thin. Looks like a classic nerd. Someone you'd see in IT, not in HR, but he has the personality for HR, apparently.

By the time our orientation tour is over, my stomach is growling. Surprising, since I haven't been hungry since Luke left.

"I'll be your lunch date today," Morgan says. "We've got reservations at The Glass House."

My heart drops into my stomach. There goes the hunger.

"Something wrong, Katelyn?" Morgan asks.

"No, of course not."

"Oh good. You just got a weird look on your face when I mentioned The Glass House."

"Did I?"

Note to self: be aware of my facial expressions at all times.

"The Glass House sounds great," Lance says. "One of my favorite places."

"Yeah," I say. "Mine too. Zee and I—"

Oops. Not the best time to be mentioning my relationship with Zee.

"I mean... Mrs. Wolfe and I..."

"Don't worry about anything, Katelyn," Morgan says. "I'm well aware of your relationship with Ms. Wolfe."

"Oh. I just don't want you to think... You know..."

"No one thinks anything."

"I think a few things," Lance says with a smile. "I think I'm hungry, and I'm very excited about going to lunch at The Glass House."

"Good," Morgan says. "Let's go down, and we'll get a cab."

The Glass House. I have to go to The Glass House. And Luke won't be there.

I'm here for a job.

Remember that, Katelyn. Remember why you're here. And don't screw this up.

21

LUKE

Everyone had a theory about Lucifer Raven.

Word on the street, according to my sources, was that he was brutally murdered by an ex-girlfriend.

Word underground, again according to my sources, was that he turned canary and was chopped up into bits and pieces by King himself.

Word in my parents' circle, according to my father, was that he went on a trip around the world staying in hostels. Doing things as if he didn't have any money. Rebelling against his blueblood upbringing. So not me.

And word on the beach was that I went out to surf...and never came back.

Reality, of course, was that I got shot, was handcuffed to a hospital bed, and then made a deal that my father brokered.

Several of my cohorts are now spending their life behind bars.

But not King.

King was too high up to get caught.

Last I heard he was in Mexico, having fled for his life after I turned on him.

But I know better.

King is here. Here in LA.

I can feel him.

Which means I'm far from safe.

I knew coming back to LA would put my life in danger. That was a given.

But now that I know King is here?

I'm not just in danger.

I've got a bullseye on my back.

I managed to get to LA without incident. My hair is still dark, and of course I wore my dark contacts. All my papers are in the name Luke Johnson, and my father sent a car to pick me up. I've been lying low in his mansion since then.

He and I have been strategizing, figuring out what to do next.

I've hated every minute of it. Having to depend on my old man—my old man who visited that damned island.

I haven't asked him about Katelyn yet. I'm frightened to. What if he says yes? That he was with Katelyn on that island?

Fuck. I hate being beholden to him.

I've got my own damned money.

But the truth is that I can't do this alone. I need someone with my old man's clout. I gave up that clout when I became Lucifer Raven.

Plus...I have something to live for now. Make that some*one*.

Katelyn has texted me a few times. I started to text her back once but then stopped. I can't. I just can't put her through thinking that I'll be home anytime soon. That we may have a chance.

Because I know the truth.

I'm a dead man.

A fucking dead man walking.

My childhood room is upstairs on the second floor.

But I'm in the basement. Not just the basement, but an old bomb shelter that is actually below the basement. My grandfather, Lucifer the first, freaked out during the Cold War and had it constructed.

Hell, I never even knew it was here until I was over thirty years old. Now that I know, I'm glad it's here. I'm safe here. Safe while I figure out my next move.

How do you redeem yourself?

How do you find yourself?

Religion?

Philosophy?

Witchcraft?

For me it's not that simple.

For me it means confronting my past—the sins of my past —and fixing things as best I can.

At least I don't have to get those derelicts out of prison. They deserve to be there.

I deserve to be there.

Perhaps that's what it's come to. Perhaps—if I manage to get out of this alive—I'll go to prison, despite my immunity.

Perhaps that's the only way for redemption—if there is even a way at all.

Prison means a life away from Katelyn.

Of course, so does death.

Then there are the women I've wronged. Emily the worst of all. In a way, I owe Emily my life. It was on Wolfe Island that I found her, and it was on Wolfe Island that I was shot in the shoulder.

Shot in the shoulder and finally caught.

Which led to where I am now.

Emily led me to Katelyn.

I can't go near Emily. She has a restraining order against me, and I don't blame her. Damn... How did I think I was in love with Emily? She's a beautiful woman, a wonderful artist, but what I felt for her... It seemed so real at the time, but now that I know true love, I know my feelings for Emily were anything but.

Her brother Buck shot me. He's the ex-Navy SEAL who also works for the Wolfes.

My life seems totally intertwined with the Wolfes now.

And if Katelyn and I ever do get a real shot at something, it will still be intertwined with the Wolfes.

What will happen when Katelyn finds out who I truly am?

Always and forever. She said she'd love me always and forever.

Will she? How could she? How will she ever be able to love me always and forever when she finds out who I truly am and what I've truly done?

I can't think about her now. If I do, I'll think about leaving. I'll think about running back to Manhattan just to be with her.

I can't do that. Not until I fix what I can.

Which may mean...ending my life.

Be honest with yourself. There's no maybe about it. Your life will *end.*

I jump when the intercom buzzes.

"Yes?" I say.

"Lucy." My mother's voice.

She's the only one who gets away with that horrendous

nickname. Everyone else calls me Trey. Except for the new people in my life who call me Luke.

"Hilly's going to bring you some breakfast."

"Thanks, Mom."

I'm not hungry.

I'll probably never be hungry again. But one thing I do know—I need my strength, so I need fuel. Which means I need to eat.

I wait five minutes and then open the door. My breakfast is on a tray sitting on the table next to the door. I pick it up and take it back into my room.

Also known as the bomb shelter.

My mother was happy to see me.

I'm her oldest. Her first baby. She always believed in me, always supported me. Even when she shouldn't have.

"I always knew you'd come back to us, Lucy," she said when I returned.

I let her embrace me, and I let her think everything would be okay.

She should know better.

An eight-ounce glass of fresh-squeezed orange juice sits on the tray. I down it in one gulp. This, I have missed.

Florida can have its orange juice. I'm California all the way. Sure, we're known for navel oranges more than juice oranges, but I swear there's nothing like fresh-squeezed California orange juice.

When I was a kid, there was this place called The Orange Ball—a little stand that served fresh-squeezed orange juice on the outskirts of the city. The tiny place seriously looked like a giant orange. I loved that place. It went out of business years ago, driven to bankruptcy by the corporate orange juice market.

I eat the bacon, the oatmeal, the two poached eggs. I slather butter and jam on my San Francisco sourdough toast and eat that too.

It all tastes the same. But at least my belly is full.

Now, to figure out what's going on.

My old man is putting out his feelers. Still, should I even trust him?

Hell, no.

Speak of the devil.

His voice comes through the intercom.

"Trey," he says. "It's time."

It's time.

That means it's time for us to begin our plan.

Am I ready? Yes, I am. I'm ready to do what I must do to be worthy of Katelyn.

I'm ready to do what I must do to be able to live with myself.

—

22

KATELYN

The Glass House looks exactly the same. The lunch menu is slightly scaled-down but virtually no different.

Morgan and Lance each order a cocktail.

"Katelyn?" Morgan nods to me.

"I'll just have water, please."

Drinking at a work lunch strikes me as not the best thing, but that's not why I refuse. I mean, if Morgan and Lance can both have a drink so can I. No one will think anything of it. The real reason I don't have a drink is because I'm thinking of Luke. Luke, who no longer drinks. Luke who is so much stronger than I can ever be.

"I'll be back with your drinks in a moment," the server says, and then he looks at me. "Have we met?"

"I don't think so."

Recognition dawns on his face. "Of course, I remember you. You were here the night Mrs. Wolfe went into labor. My name is Travis. I'm Luke's friend. He was your waiter that night."

Now what? "Yes, that was quite a night," I say.

"How's Mrs. Wolfe doing?"

"She's good. The baby's good."

"That's great to hear. I'll get the drinks started now." Travis whisks away from the table.

"You seem to know everyone here," Lance says.

"I just happened to be here on a very eventful night," I reply.

"Have you seen the baby?" Morgan asks.

I nod. "She's beautiful."

"I can't imagine she wouldn't be with Mr. and Mrs. Wolfe as her parents," Morgan says.

Lance glances at the menu. "Apparently you've been here before, Katelyn. What do you recommend?"

"Didn't you just say this is one of your favorite places? I should probably ask you what you recommend."

"From the lunch menu, I like the salmon."

"I don't eat seafood," I say.

"You don't?"

"It's a long story."

"Morgan and I have an hour. Care to enlighten us?"

My cheeks warm, and my heart begins to race. Nerves. It's just nerves. The truth? I can't tell them why I don't like seafood. That I was force-fed fish on the island, and now everything about the water reminds me of that place.

"Allergic," I say quickly.

"Are you having an allergic reaction now?" Morgan asks.

"Not that I know of. Why?" I try to control my breathing. In. Out. In. Out.

"Your cheeks are red," he says.

I swallow and then rise, nearly knocking over my chair. "Excuse me."

I walk as calmly as I can to the women's room. As soon as I'm safely inside, I grab the first counter I see. The reflection in the mirror tells the tale. My cheeks are blazing. My heart is still beating quickly—so quickly I can actually see my chest move.

I'm not scared. So why am I having a panic attack?

Macy would say it's because I was asked a question about the fish. She's probably right.

Maybe it's time to call Macy for a one-on-one session. Except when? I'm working full time now. Maybe she could see me on my lunch hour.

I go into a stall, even though I don't have to go to the bathroom. I just want to hide from the world. Hide from the mirror.

Hide from myself.

How am I going to get through all of this?

Sometimes it seems so doable, but then sometimes... Times like this...

The smallest thing—like explaining why I don't eat seafood—sends me into a tailspin.

I work hard to regulate my breathing, and then I leave the stall. I wash my hands. My cheeks are still red, but at least they're not on fire.

Are you okay? That's the question that will greet me when I get back to the table with Morgan and Lance.

I must come up with some kind of reasonable explanation.

And I must come up with it quickly, because the longer I stay in here, the more likely they're going to send someone in after me.

What can I tell them? An upset stomach? No. They'll tell

me to go home instead of going back to the office. Not what I want on my first day.

I pull my phone out of my purse. If I'm holding my phone... Yes, that's it.

I hastily walk back to the table.

"Everything okay?" Morgan asks.

"Yes," I say. "Sorry I left in such a hurry, but I got a text from my mother. My father's in surgery today for a liver biopsy. I just didn't want to be here in case it was bad news."

"And...?" Lance asks.

"Good news so far."

"I'm happy to hear that," Morgan says.

I take my seat. My water has been delivered, and I take a sip.

One bullet dodged.

How am I going to keep this up?

I glance at the menu. Since I don't eat a lot of red meat, and seafood is a bust, poultry is usually my go-to. Either that or the vegetarian or vegan option.

Pasta. Pasta always works. As long as it's not pasta with frutti di mare.

Pasta with lemon and basil. That looks amazing. I close my menu.

"You decided?" Lance says.

"Pasta with lemon and basil."

"Sounds yummy," Lance says, "but I'm a lot hungrier than that. I'm going to have the salmon with a Caesar salad."

"That sounds great," Morgan says. "I'll have the same." He glances at Lance.

Oh. I know that look.

Morgan has the hots for our lunch companion.

The only problem is that Lance isn't gay. If he were, he wouldn't have given me his card the other day on the street.

Morgan will find out soon enough.

The two of them seem to have an easy rapport, though. Which is good because it means I don't have to do a lot of talking.

Every few minutes, one of them asks me a question. I give a two- or three-word answer, and they continue with their conversation.

Works for me.

My pasta is delicious, though I'm still not very hungry. Still, I force myself to finish the entire plateful. If I'm going to do a job and do it well, I need to be nourished.

I look at my phone sitting beside my plate.

I lied about getting a call from my mom. I haven't heard from her yet. We won't know the biopsy results for a day or two anyway. My father's strong. He'll get through the surgery with no problem. I know this, so I'm not freaked in the slightest when an actual text comes in from my mother.

I don't run to the bathroom, as I did when I got the fake text.

Morgan and Lance are deep in conversation, so I simply pick up my phone and look at it.

And then I gasp.

Jorge Herrera owns a chain of taco shops called Los Tacos. They've been voted the best tacos in LA for ten years straight, and they are fucking delicious.

His seasoning for the ground beef is a closely held secret. All the biggest chefs in LA have tried to replicate it, but with no luck.

Jorge is a multimillionaire. His taco business is great, but it didn't make him millions.

Jorge moves drugs.

And the man who got him started?

Yours truly.

KING TAKES *me aside a year after he brought me into the business.*

"Listen, Raven," King says, "you've proven your loyalty. But there's still more you have to do if you want to move up in this organization."

"Just say the word," I say.

"We need a front. A new front. The Chicken Shack is going under."

I lift my eyebrows. The Chicken Shack has been moving drugs for the last several years, according to King.

"What happened?"

"The DEA raided one of their trucks. Found four hundred kilos of meth."

"Shit."

"You're telling me. So we need a new partner."

"Yeah, I guess we do."

"That's where you come in."

"Me?"

"Yeah, you. You have contacts. Contacts with big business."

"Big business isn't going to get involved in this. You know that, King."

"You'd be surprised what big business gets into, but it doesn't necessarily need to be one of the Fortune 500."

"Oh?"

"Yeah. I need you to find us a new front. Someone who's trustworthy. Someone who's hungry."

"I'll see what I can do."

"You take care of this, Raven, and you can write your own fucking ticket."

It's kismet that I have a hankering for tacos later that day. I stop at Jorge's Beverly Hills location, and Jorge is there himself.

"Mr. Ashton," Jorge says, stopping at my table. "Great to see you. How is your food?"

"Delicious as always, Jorge."

"If there's anything you need, you just let me know."

I nod.

When I'm finished with my lunch, I rise to go throw out the trash, when I decide to order a few more tacos to go. I head to the *counter, passing Jorge, who is having a conversation on his cell phone.*

"Not possible," I hear Jorge say. "You need to give me more time, bro."

I pull out my own phone, feign checking for messages, as I listen to Jorge.

"No, man, that'll cost me my business. You can't do this to me."

I shove my phone back in my pocket, go to the counter, place an order for four more tacos to go. Once they're bagged, and I'm walking out of the store, I sidetrack Jorge.

"You want to talk?" I ask.

"Sure, what do you need, Mr. Ashton?"

"It's not what I need, Jorge. It's what you need. And no more of this Mr. Ashton stuff. Call me Raven."

JORGE IS STILL WORKING for King. I know that because all his locations are still thriving. I'm the one who made it happen. I made Jorge Herrera a rich man.

I never gave up his name.

The FBI and the DEA weren't interested in small potatoes like Jorge. They wanted big names. They wanted the kings.

I gave them King's name. knowing what it would cost me potentially. And even though word on the street is that he hightailed it to Mexico, I know better.

He's here.

And I think I need to get some tacos.

Am I unrecognizable enough? The brown hair and brown eyes hide my true identity well. But this is LA. This is where people know the Ashton family.

This is where the underground knows Lucifer Raven.

I've been hiding in the stupid bomb shelter for days now, and that's been long enough.

It's time to do what I came for.

Attempt to redeem myself.

Jorge is as good of a place to begin as anything.

I head to the bathroom, touch up my blond roots with hair color, shave off two days of blond stubble. After a shower, I dress in board shorts and a long-sleeved T-shirt. Then I put an LA Dodgers baseball cap on my head.

Just another beach bum.

I walk up to the basement and then up to the main floor of our Beverly Hills mansion. I manage to escape the staff, and I'm nearly out the door when—

"Lucy, where are you going?"

My mother.

My gorgeous blond and blue-eyed mother, who looks the exact same way as she did when I was a kid. It's not Beverly Hills plastic surgery, it's just Mom. She's that beautiful.

"Just to get some tacos," I say.

She looks me over. "You don't look like yourself."

"That's the point, Mom."

"Your father said you're not to leave the house yet. He said you two are working on a plan, and that—"

"Mom, I have to. I'm here for a reason."

"Of course you are. You've come home. We need to protect you."

"I don't deserve your protection, Mom. You know that as well as I do."

"Lucy, you're my baby. My first baby. I will never turn my back on you. Not ever."

"You know what I've done. You know who I am."

"You're absolutely right. I know you've done horrible

things. But you're also right when you say I know who you are. You're my child—my sweet, beautiful firstborn child. I know there is good in your heart."

She's not wrong. There's a lot of good in my heart. Especially now, since I got off the alcohol and since I've been to therapy. Since I've realized the things I did were not just wrong but unforgivable. And that's the whole issue.

"There *is* good in my heart," I tell her.

"That's all I need to know." She pulls me to her and embraces me.

For moment I'm a little boy again, getting comfort in my mother's arms.

I let myself succumb to her loving warmth for a moment.

But only a moment.

I pull away. "I love you, Mom. But I have to do this." I head to the door of the mansion and walk through it.

24

KATELYN

"Everything okay?" Lance asks.

"It's my mother again," I say. "There's an issue with my father's surgery after all."

I read the text again.

Call me right away. It's about your father's surgery.

"Could you excuse me? I need to make a quick call to my mother."

"Of course," Morgan says. "We're done here anyway. Go ahead, and I'll take care of the check."

"Thank you." I rise and walk through the restaurant to the doorway. Once I'm outside on the busy sidewalk, I walk around to the back of the restaurant.

The alley. The alley where Luke and I...

It's a little quieter back here, but was this really the best idea to come back here to make a phone call?

A dog wanders up to me. He's a little scruffy but adorable with short light hair.

"Hey." I kneel to pet him. "You must be Jed."

With Luke gone, is anyone feeding him? He looks hungry.

"I'll find you some food," I promise. "Right after I make a call, okay?"

His big brown eyes gaze at me, and for a moment, I'm sure he understands me.

I quickly make a call to my mother.

"Katelyn?" she says frantically.

"Yeah, it's me. What's wrong?"

"Your father... He had a reaction to the anesthesia or something. They're not quite sure what, but he's..." She chokes out a sob.

"Mom, what's wrong? Tell me what's wrong with Dad."

"He's in a coma," she says. "And I don't know... I don't know how to get through this, Katelyn."

My heart thumps wildly as fear tries to strangle me. Not my father. Not after everything else.

"If you can possibly come," she says. "I understand about your new job, but..."

She's not lying, is she? My mother's capable of a lot of things, but she wouldn't lie to me about my father. Right?

"May I speak to the doctor?"

"He's not here right now."

"Mom, before I pack my life up and come to LA, leave a new job I just started today, I really would like to talk to the doctor."

"I can't believe this. You think I'm not telling you the truth."

"It's not that at all. But please understand, I have people depending on me. I just started the new job *today*."

"All right. Hold on. I'll try to find him."

I have no idea how long I'll be standing here behind the restaurant, waiting for my mother to get back on the phone with the doctor. Heck, she could have someone pretend to be a doctor and tell me what I want to hear.

I'd call the hospital myself, except I don't know which hospital, and there are a ton of hospitals in LA. I have no choice. I have to stay here, looking into Jed's sad brown eyes and waiting for my mother to get back on the phone.

I sit down on the ground, knowing full well I may be staining my clothes. I pet Jed's soft head. He's a little thin. "Hey, buddy. I'm going to take care of you."

Something hits me in the heart then. This dog is mine. He's going home with me. Am I allowed to have a dog at my place? I don't even care. I need this dog, and he needs me.

He makes me feel closer to Luke.

Plus...my mom never let me have a dog when I was a kid.

"I promise you, Jed," I say, "you'll never be hungry—"

"Katelyn?" My mother's voice is breathless.

"Yeah, I'm here."

"I found an intern. She's going to tell you what's going on."

"All right."

Then, a new voice. "Ms. Brooks?"

"Yes, this is Katelyn Brooks."

"I'm Dr. Shelby, one of the interns on your father's case."

"Who's his attending physician?"

"Dr. Mark Lindstrom, but he's on another case right now. I've been with your father through everything, and I can tell you what's going on."

"All right, thank you. Is he going to be okay?"

"Right now, his vitals are stable, and he doesn't appear to be in any immediate danger, but he is in a coma."

"What exactly does that mean, doctor?"

"It means he's not waking from the anesthesia. However, his brain activity seems to be okay."

"Is this normal?"

"I'll be honest with you, Ms. Brooks. It's not usual. Most patients have no trouble returning to consciousness after anesthesia, but it does happen."

"My mother wants me to come out. I'm in Manhattan and I just started a new job. Tell me, and please be honest. Is my father in any danger?"

"His life is not in danger at the moment. However, if he doesn't come out of the coma on his own, you and your mother will have to make a decision."

"A decision?"

"Yes. Whether to end his life support. Donate his organs. That kind of thing."

My heart drops into my stomach.

Sure, I knew this was coming, but still... It's like a lead brick. To actually hear a doctor say the words.

"Don't tell her that!" I hear my mother snap in the background.

"Mrs. Brooks, you told me to tell her the truth."

"I know, but for God's sake. End life support?"

"That's far into the future, ma'am, but she asked me to tell her the truth."

"For God's sake, give me the phone." A pause. "Katelyn?"

"Hi, Mom."

"Don't listen to a word she says. She's a quack. Your father will be fine."

"Then you don't need me to come out after all?"

"No, that's not what I meant. Of course I need you. Your father's in a coma, for God's sake."

Dear Lord. Which one of my mother's personalities is going to take the reins here?

"Mom, I'll do what I can. But if they won't give me time off work—"

"They will give you time off work. If they don't, they are horrible, terrible people."

I already know the Wolfes will be sympathetic. I'm the problem. I love my father. Even my mother.

But how can I let the Wolfes down?

Then again...

Luke is in LA.

But no.

I must be strong. I will talk to the Wolfes. I will tell them everything. I quickly end the call with my mother.

"I'll be back for you, Jed," I promise my four-legged friend. "I'm going to get you some food and a leash, and then I'm taking you home."

Yes, Jed is coming home with me.

To Manhattan.

And to LA.

25

LUKE

I place my order for five tacos and then ask, "Is Jorge around?"

"He's not at this location today," the guy behind the counter says.

Shit. "Can you tell me where he is?"

"I'm not sure." He doesn't move.

"Well...could you check?"

"Yeah, sure," he says in monotone.

I may have to talk to Jorge about the guys he hires. This dude hardly has customer service written all over his face.

Despite the line of people behind me, counter guy does go to the back. The manager returns.

"You're looking for Jorge?" she says.

"Yes, Maralee," I say, eyeing her tag and smiling. "He's an old friend. Do you know where I can find him today?"

"I think he's at the warehouse," she says. "We're expecting a shipment of taco shells."

"Thanks." I smile again, take my tacos to go, and head to my car.

Eating a taco while you're driving is a learned art. I've got it down. I polish off all five tacos before I get to the Los Tacos warehouse.

This is where it all happens. This is where product is loaded and unloaded. Not just food product, but drug product.

The fact that Jorge is here today means drugs are most likely coming in.

Man, is he even going to want to speak to me? He knows I ratted out some higher-ups.

A couple of truckers are standing in the shade behind the warehouse having a cigarette and a Pepsi.

"Hey," I say to them. "I'm looking for Jorge. He here?"

"Inside," one of them says, stamping his cigarette out in the grass.

"Thanks."

I walk inside, and I truly have no idea what awaits me. No one seems to recognize me, which is good. Jorge has an office near the front of the building, and that's where I head.

I knock on the door.

"Yeah?"

"I need to talk to Jorge," I say.

"Who is it?"

"A friend."

Silence.

Then Jorge opens the door. "Do I know you?"

"You do," I say.

Recognition dawns on his face. It must be my voice.

"You've got to be shitting me," he says.

I walk inside his office, uninvited, and close the door. "We good in here?"

"Yeah, we are."

I trust him. I trusted that we are not being listened to or watched. Still, I do a quick scan around for surveillance. No cameras that I can see. Listening devices are another thing altogether. They could be anywhere. But I choose to trust Jorge.

"Lucifer fucking Raven." He walks behind his desk and sits down.

"Yeah, it's me."

"We all thought you were dead."

"I probably should be."

"What are you doing here?"

"Trying to right some wrongs."

"And you came here?"

"Yeah. I got you into this mess, Jorge."

"What mess? I'm doing great."

"You mean you don't want out?"

"Why would I?"

"Because the DEA could come in and close you down at any time."

"I'm very careful."

"I'm just giving you a chance to get out," I say. "I got you into it."

"I'm a big boy, Raven. I made my own decision all those years ago. Sure, you gave me the opportunity, but I could've said no. Hell, I could have called the DEA on you right then."

He's not wrong.

Of course, no one could've touched me. At that time, I was still protected by the Ashton name, and I was fast becoming King's right-hand man, so I had his protection as well.

"Look," I say. "I've had a major change of heart. I've got a hell of a lot of red on my ledger, and I want to mark off as much as I can."

"I'm not interested. I like my life the way it is."

"What if I finance a move for you? Get you the hell out of the country?"

"If I want to leave the country, I'll finance it myself."

"Not if the Feds seize your assets."

Jorge rises then, stares me down. "What the fuck are you not telling me, Raven?"

"Nothing. You have nothing to fear from me. I'll never turn you in. But a lot of other people know about you, Jorge. I'm offering you the chance to get out while you can."

"Why? You got me into this. Why would you want me to get out? Surely you're making a lot of—" His jaw drops. "You're on the run, aren't you?"

"Not really. Not anymore, anyway, though I would appreciate it you didn't mention that you saw me."

"I owe you a lot. Of course you have my word."

"And you have mine. No one will hear about you from me. Are you sure I can't tempt you?"

"No. I got a system worked out. I'm protected."

"What about the people who work for you?"

"They're paid handsomely to keep their mouths shut."

"I know that. But even if they can't get to you, they might be able to get to your people."

"My people understand the risks when they get in. They're all set up so that their families will be taken care of if any of them go down."

King took good care of Jorge. Just like he took good care of me all those years.

Hell, I'd probably still be in this life if Buck Moreno hadn't shot me.

A twinge erupts in my shoulder where the bullet struck.

In its way, that gunshot was the best thing that ever happened to me.

I was caught.

I had no choice but to make a deal. Without a deal, I'd be rotting in prison right now. Or be dead on the street, killed by King himself.

I trust very few people in this business. Jorge Herrera is one of them.

He won't alert anyone that I'm back in town.

I wish he would take my offer. He has a wife and kids. People who depend on him. Funny how I didn't consider any of this all those years ago when I made him the offer.

Things change. *I've* changed.

"What can I say to make you change your mind?" I ask.

"Nothing. Go on your way, Raven. No one will know you were here."

26

KATELYN

"Please," Reid says. "Stop apologizing. It's okay. You need to go home and tend to your father."

"I just feel awful. On the first day of a new job."

"This job will still be here when you get back."

"That's just the thing," I say. "I don't know how long I'm going to be gone. I can't expect you to go without a personal assistant for all that time."

"I've been going without a personal assistant since I fired Terrence almost a year ago," he says. "I've been making do with temps, and Alicia and others have been picking up the slack. This isn't a big deal, Katelyn."

"It's a big deal to me."

"I understand. I totally appreciate your reluctance to leave me in a lurch. But the most important thing to me and to Zee is that you heal fully. That means being there for your father as well as dealing with the rest of your life."

"I suppose this must be a first for you," I say. "An employee to ask for leave of absence on the first day."

He smiles then. "I can't say that it's happened before, but your circumstances are definitely unique."

I sigh. "I can't thank you enough for this."

"No thanks are needed. Take care of family first. I would do the same."

I rise, smile, and shake Reid's outstretched hand. "I'll keep you posted."

"Yes, please do. And if there's anything you need. Anything your father needs. You know you can just call us."

I nod and leave his office.

I could probably ask these people for anything, and they'd give it to me. My father is in the tech business, so I know he has good health insurance. I won't need to ask.

First things first. I head into a pet store and pick up some dog food, a collar, a leash, and a traveling kennel. I drop my purchases off at home and then head back out with the collar, leash, and a cup of dog food secured in a zippered plastic bag.

When I get to the alley behind The Glass House, Jed is nowhere to be found.

Now what? I'm leaving for LA tomorrow, and I want to take the dog with me. I need him as much as he needs me.

I lean against the wall.

This is where Luke first kissed me. I wasn't ready. I'm still not ready. But the passion and the chemistry with Luke... I didn't expect it.

I didn't expect anything so sudden and so provocative. So personal and so necessary.

"I miss you," I say aloud.

I close my eyes.

I miss him so much. Why hasn't he called me? Or at least texted me?

I sigh and open my eyes.

Jed is sitting in front of me.

His beautiful brown doggy eyes are staring at me with wonder and pleading.

I kneel and pet his soft face. "There you are, baby. I'm so glad you showed up." I pull the dog food out of my bag and pour it onto the ground for Jed. He greedily snarfs it up, and I wish I'd brought some water.

While he's busy eating, I slip the collar and leash around his neck.

He resists at first, but I get him to come with me. Then I take a cab back to my place.

Security stops me, of course.

"Ms. Brooks, I'm not sure about a dog."

"Is there a hard-and-fast rule?"

"I don't think so, but—"

"Don't worry about it. I'm leaving to go visit my parents in LA tomorrow. He'll only be here for one night."

"And then he'll be staying in LA?" the security officer says.

"I don't know. Maybe. Maybe not."

I don't know what I'm going to do. I've got a job here, and I've got security here.

I've got the Wolfes. Zee and Reid especially.

And little Nora. I'm supposed to be her godmother at her baptism in a few months.

I can always fly back for that.

I'll return. This is my home now.

Except...

Luke.

"Come on," I say to Jed.

"Is that dog housebroken?" the officer asks.

"I don't know. I'll clean up after him. We're leaving tomorrow. Please."

"All right." The security officer shakes his head. "I'd better not hear any barking."

"He'll be fine."

At least I hope he will be. I don't know anything about dogs, and Jed's a stray. He's not used to following directions. What if he does make a lot of noise?

Doesn't matter.

He's mine.

Mine and Luke's.

I will not let him down. If I let Jed down, it would be like letting Luke down. I can't do it. Besides, I'm already in love with the little mutt.

"First things first," I say to Jed. "You need a drink of water. Then a bath."

Giving Jed a bath proves to be a challenge. I get more suds on me than the dog. But I'm laughing. I'm laughing and having fun. When I try to dry him off, only for him to escape the towel and shake water droplets everywhere, I laugh some more. What a mess!

Well, I wanted a dog.

But Jed is wagging his tail, panting, and...smiling. I know dogs can't actually smile, but I swear Jed is full of joy.

His belly is full, and he's clean for the first time in...well, probably a long time.

"Welcome to your new life, Jed." I laugh as he kisses my face. "I hate the thought of putting you in that kennel and taking you on the plane, but it will only be a few hours. Then we'll be reunited in LA."

I put out some more water for Jed and then begin to pack my stuff. After a quick Internet search on how best to prepare your dog for flight, I take as much of their advice as I can and make sure Jed is ready for tomorrow's grand adventure.

Mom doesn't know I'm bringing a dog home to her sparkling clean house. I don't care. I won't stay in my old room anyway. I'll stay in the guesthouse.

I'll probably be spending a lot of time at the hospital until we figure out what's going on with my father, but the guesthouse has a fenced-in yard that will be perfect for Jed. I'll just have to make sure there's enough shade because it gets so hot in LA.

Once I'm packed and after I've made myself a sandwich and eaten it, I wash up and go to bed.

Jed climbs up on the bed next to me.

A dog has no place on a bed, I can hear my mother saying.

I smile as I pet his clean, soft coat. "I'm glad you're here, Jed. I'm so glad you're here."

27

LUKE

I'm so tired of long-sleeved shirts.

I should've tried to get the tattoo removed. It was on my list, but then I met Katelyn.

But who am I kidding? Even if the tattoo were gone, I would still be Lucifer Raven. I can't escape who I truly am.

"There are some things I can't fix," I say to myself. "I guess I'm going to have to live with that."

Coming back here to make amends—to get the red off my ledger—was a silly idea. I can't make amends. All I can do is learn from my mistakes and try to live the straight and narrow from now on.

If only I truly were Luke Johnson—no man and every man.

But I'm not. I'm Lucifer Charles Ashton III, otherwise known as Lucifer Raven.

I'm truly a dead man walking.

I remember when I first saw Emily Moreno. Dark hair and dark eyes so different from the blond and blue-eyed women who usually crowd the LA beaches. She was painting.

Painting on a canvas, while all the other women sunbathed or drank drinks with umbrellas in them.

I was drawn to her immediately.

Back then, I had no problem wearing short sleeves or tank tops. For those who knew who I was, the tattoo reminded them not to cross me. And those who didn't? It made me look pretty badass.

Back then I had long blond hair. Sometimes I wore it in a low ponytail and sometimes in a messy man bun. Other times, when it wasn't quite so hot, I let it flow over my shoulders.

My old man hated my hair long like that, and I think my mom did too, though she never said anything.

"You've got a lot of talent," I say to Emily.

"Oh. Thank you. I'm sorry, I didn't see you."

"I'm sure you didn't. You were engrossed in your work."

She turns then and looks at me, her eyebrows rising. The reaction I get from women is unusual. They all stare for a moment.

Sometimes I think it's the hair. Or maybe it's just that I'm good-looking and muscular.

"That's some really cool ink," she says, eyeing my left arm.

"Thanks."

"You have any other tattoos?"

"That's the only one."

"It's amazing. You don't see a lot of people with something that ornate unless they're inked up all over the place."

"I never really thought about getting another one," I say.

She smiles. "Not the name of some woman?"

"No. I've seen too many guys get somebody tattooed on their body and then have a bad breakup."

"I see."

I don't ask her out that day.

But the next day, when I go back to the beach, and she's painting again, I ask her for a drink.

Two weeks later, she moves into my beach house.

I FELL hard and fast that time.

Just like I did with Katelyn.

But there was one thing I couldn't do for Emily or any other woman that I'm going to do for Katelyn today, and only one person I trust to do it.

My brother.

Sebastian Ashton. Not a joke. He hated being saddled with that, but I had no sympathy for him. Hell, at least he wasn't named after the devil himself.

And I'm not talking about Satan. I'm talking about our father.

My brother was as big of a disappointment to our father as I was.

No, he didn't become a criminal, but he did take his trust fund once he turned twenty-one and open a tattoo parlor on the beach.

He and I were never close, but we are blood.

He didn't do my left arm.

Still wearing long sleeves in this wretched heat, I take one of my father's many cars and drive to Sebastian's place.

I walk in.

"Can I help you?" a tattooed, gum-popping receptionist asks.

"I'm looking for Bas. Is he here?"

"In the back. Working on some art.

"Can you get him for me?"

"I could, but who are you?"

"I'm his..."

What do I tell her? Jorge knows I'm back in town, but he's the only one. I trust him. Hell, he won't rat me out. Ratting me out would be ratting himself out.

But I can't hide forever.

"I'm his brother."

"You don't look much like him."

Actually, I do. He's blond and blue-eyed, but of course right now I'm brown-haired and brown-eyed.

"Just tell him," I say. "He'll see me."

"Okay." She gets up and walks, slowly, into the back. The zing of the electric needle rents through the air when she opens the door.

I looked down at my left arm covered in cloth. Damn, it took five different sessions to get my Raven perfect.

Here goes nothing.

"He says to wait here."

I jerk. I didn't even hear the receptionist come back.

"Okay."

She nods to a few chairs. "Sit there. He'll be out as soon as he can."

"How many people are back there?" I ask.

"Just Bas and his client."

"Do any other artists work here?"

"A few, but only Bas is here today."

Good. I lucked out. I don't really want to see anyone other than my brother.

I skim through some of his books. I don't have anything overly intricate in mind for today. Just a simple name.

Katelyn.

Nothing flowery or girly. Just her name. So she'll always be with me, no matter what.

My brother walks through the door then.

His hair is blond, and it covers his ears. He never wore it quite as long as I did, but neither of us are clean-cut.

He looks me in the eye, and I can't quite read his expression. Does he believe it's me?

"Come on back," he says gruffly.

Damn, his voice sounds so much like mine. Low and husky. Must've come from our mother's side, because our father doesn't sound anything like either one of us.

I stand, not glancing at the receptionist, and follow my brother.

"Where's your client?" I ask.

"I sent him out the back door."

"Good. Thanks."

He stares at me, gazes into my eyes. "It's really you, Trey?"

"Hair color and contacts," I say.

"You motherfucker," he says. "I thought you were dead."

"I know. I'm sorry, bro."

"Don't even. Sandy and I were beside ourselves."

"You were not." I hold back a scoff.

"Okay, so we aren't close. You're still my fucking brother. You're still Sandy's brother. We thought you were gone forever."

"I kind of thought I was too."

"What the fuck, man? Where have you been?"

"It's a long, boring story."

"Yeah, I'm pretty sure it's long. But boring? Sell it to the Air Force. I'm not buying."

"Look," I say. "The less you know, the safer you are."

"The old man helped you, didn't he?"

I stay silent. I've no lost love for my father, but there's no reason to finger him to his other son. At least not yet.

"I came in here to get a tattoo," I say.

"You planning on paying me?"

"I'll pay you whatever you want, Bas. It's a simple woman's name. That's all."

"A woman's name on your skin, Trey?" He scoffs. "I don't fucking believe it."

"Yeah, well, things change."

"Tell you what. I'll tattoo a woman's name all over the cheeks of your ass if you want. I won't charge you a damned penny. Except...you need to level with me."

"First, you're not going anywhere near my ass. And second, I've got nothing to say."

"That's bullshit and we both know it."

"You're better off not knowing. You know that."

He doesn't reply for a minute.

Yeah, he's thinking. He's thinking I'm right, which I am.

"What are you doing back here?" he finally asks. "You've got to have a target bigger than the *Titanic* on your back."

"You're not wrong. But I've got some things to take care of. I've change, Bas."

Another scoff from my brother.

That's okay. I don't expect him to believe me. Hell, I wouldn't believe me if I were him.

"Don't make me tell you," I say. "I don't want you in danger. You or Sandy or Mom."

"What about Dad?"

Tough call. What can I say? Having learned from Pollack that our father frequented Derek Wolfe's Island, I'm not sure I care what happens to him.

Pollack could be lying, of course, but why would he?

"Our father's not the man you think he is," I say.

"I never thought he was some hero, Trey. You know that."

"Yeah? Well, suffice it to say he may be worse than any of us ever thought."

"I know who the bastard is," Sebastian says. "I was the one left, remember? After you died—er, disappeared—he turned on me. I had to protect Sandy."

Our sister, Alexandra—nicknamed Sandy—is five years younger than I am, and a year older than Sebastian. Even though she's older, Sebastian felt responsible, protective. Kind of the way I always felt about our mother.

"Do you want an apology?" I ask. "I can apologize to the moon and back, but it won't change what I did. Those years I was gone, leaving you and Sandy to fend for yourself."

"I don't need an apology from you, Trey. I got over that a long time ago. I just want to know where the fuck you've been."

There is no easy answer to the question.

And even if there were, I can't burden my brother with it.

"Just ink me, man." I say. "Please."

28

KATELYN

"You brought home a dog?" My mother shakes her head.

I let Jed out of his kennel, and he runs through the house, nearly knocking over one of my mother's prized vases. I secretly wish the ugly thing were in pieces on the floor, but Jed misses it by a couple inches.

"You wanted me home," I say. "I come with a dog now."

My father ended up coming out of the coma while I was in flight, and now we're waiting for the liver biopsy results. My father is good, but we won't know whether he has cancer for another twenty-four hours yet.

"He can't stay here," Mom says.

"Then I won't stay here," I say. "Good enough."

My mother purses her lips. A classic Farrah Lowenstein Brooks facial expression.

I simply lift my eyebrows. I don't have a problem leaving. I don't have a ton of money, but the Wolfes give me several months of living expenses. I can afford a cheap hotel.

"He'll have to stay outside," my mother says.

"You don't have to worry about him at all. I plan to stay in the guesthouse."

"I'm afraid that's not possible. It hasn't been cleaned in ages."

"Then I'll clean it. Jed and I will stay in the guesthouse, and you won't have to be bothered with him or his shedding hair or him knocking over your imitation Ming Dynasty vases."

My mother drops her jaw.

She's not used to me talking to her like this.

"Katelyn," she says, "I'm so sorry about everything you've been through."

"You've said that to me already, Mom. I don't need to hear it anymore. What happened to me was not your fault."

"I never thought it was."

Again, classic Farrah.

"Very well, then," she says. "I'll have Casey take your bag and that...kennel...to the guesthouse."

"Thank you." I kneel to pet Jed. "You hear that, baby? We're going to have our own house out back. The guesthouse. Where you can run around all you want."

"He can't just have his run of the property," Mom says.

"I know that, Mother. But the yard is fenced, isn't it?"

"Of course."

"Then he'll be absolutely fine. And don't worry. I will scoop up all his poop, and you will never even know he's there."

"Good." She wrinkles her nose.

"Well, your grandma is just not being nice to you, is she?" I say to my puppy. "She will learn to love you just as I do."

"Don't hold your breath," Mom murmurs.

"Yes, she doesn't think we heard that, but we did, didn't we?"

"For God's sake, Katelyn, you're making me sick talking baby talk to that animal."

"Well then, Grandma will be sick for a while, because I don't plan to stop." I give Jed a kiss on his forehead.

Casey, my parents' butler, enters and clears his throat. "Hello, Miss Katelyn."

My mother and father don't have a lot of help. A butler and housekeeper. Casey does the cooking. Then of course the pool guy, but he's not full time. And the gardener.

"Hello, Casey. I'll be staying in the guesthouse."

"Yes, ma'am." He picks up my suitcase and the dog's kennel. "I'll just take these things out for you."

AN HOUR LATER, Jed and I are settled in the guesthouse. It's a lovely little bungalow, two bedrooms, two baths, and a two-car garage. I don't have a car, of course, but Mom left one for my use. The big yard is perfect for Jed.

"Well, Jed," I say, "I guess we clean this place. But first I need to go see my father in the hospital. You're going to have to be good. No chewing up all kinds of stuff while I'm gone."

I scratch him behind the ears and then drive to the hospital.

My father is asleep when I get there.

"Daddy?"

His eyes flutter open. "Katelyn. I'm so glad you made it."

"How are you feeling?"

"All right. Groggy. That stuff they gave me yesterday for the biopsy threw me for a loop."

"I know. You scared us."

"No reason to be scared. Not yet anyway."

"So the results are expected back tomorrow?"

"Later today or tomorrow, yes."

"I'll sit here with you for a while. Go back to sleep. You need your rest."

"No. I want to talk to you." But he closes his eyes.

My father and I have never had a lot to say to each other. "We'll talk later," I say. "You sleep."

He doesn't fight me this time. I pull out my phone.

Now, to find Luke. Of course there are no less than a million Luke Johnsons in the LA area. I may be exaggerating, but only a little. How am I going to find him?

I've already texted him, telling him I'm here.

And as usual, no response.

He loves me. I have to believe he loves me. He promised to call as soon as he can.

Which means only one thing.

He's not responding because he can't.

Chills skitter up my spine.

What can I do? It's not like I can scour every part of LA and find him. That would be impossible. I don't have enough money to hire a private investigator.

But my mother and father do.

I can't ask them—not when my father's waiting for biopsy results.

I should be more worried about my dad than I am. I'm concerned, yes, but I can't forget the fact that my mother told me cancer is unlikely—the reason I chose not to come in the first place.

When he didn't wake up from the anesthesia yesterday, I

was scared, but would I have run out here if Luke weren't here?

Probably not. Probably not because the Wolfes are depending on me.

I'm totally letting them down.

I feel like crap about it, but I'm here now. I'll miss group with Macy, a private session that I set up, more coffee with Aspen. My new job, which, even though I don't know what I'm doing, proved to be pretty enjoyable the first day.

I look at my father, his eyes closed, his sandy brownish-gray hair slicked back from his forehead. He doesn't look weak. He looks like the dad I remember, except he could use a shampoo.

Should he really be this tired after a liver biopsy? Surgery is surgery, so probably yes.

I get back to my phone. I search for Luke Johnson.

I don't find the one I'm looking for.

But then...I get a text.

It's from Luke.

It's a photo. A photo of his shoulder.

A new tattoo.

It says *Katelyn*.

29

LUKE

Just a photo. A photo of my new tattoo. That's all I send to Katelyn.

She knows I'm okay now. And she knows I still love her.

Funny. Either my brother has the gentlest tattoo hand in the world, or this tattoo was meant to be part of me.

I swear it didn't hurt at all.

I remember wincing through all the sessions for my raven. I thought my freaking arm was going to fall off at one point.

This time, though? It felt like it was licked on by puppies.

That silly old stray, Jed, pops in my mind then. I should call Travis. Make sure he's feeding Jed.

Damn. I've gone soft. Since when do I care about an old stray dog?

Since I got off the sauce. Since I started doing an honest day's work. And since I found Katelyn.

I'm back at the bomb shelter, standing in front of my mirror. Sebastian did something else for me besides just giving me a new tattoo. He gave me a product that he carries in the store. Tattoo cover-up. Heavy makeup that will cover the raven on my left arm and shoulder.

I stand naked in front of my mirror and slather the thick substance over my arm. Oddly, it's not as heavy as I expected. And damn...it does cover the tat.

"Will it sweat off in this heat?" I asked Bas yesterday.

"No, it shouldn't. It's totally waterproof too. This is top-of-the-line crap."

It will be nice not to have to wear long sleeves all the time.

I feel like a surf. Man, it's been a long time. I used to be great on the waves, until...

Until I got involved in the drug industry, and then my beach bum days were over.

Still, I lived on the beach. I still own that damned house.

Time to sell it, I guess.

It was bought with dirty money.

Part of my deal with the Feds was that I got to keep the house. Most of my drug money had to be handed over, but I still have my trust fund from the Ashtons.

Yep, I'm a freaking multimillionaire.

I don't give a shit about any of it.

I tried with Jorge. Wasn't able to fix that.

I'm not sure what else I can do.

There was one guy—a guy I put a hit on. I'd like to say he deserved it, but he didn't. He didn't deserve anything good, but he also didn't deserve to die. All this time I've tried to tell myself that the world is better without all those scumbags. Maybe it is, but the truth remains.

No one deserves to die.

It took therapy and getting off alcohol for me to understand that.

The guy left alone a wife and a baby. I'm talking to an attorney this afternoon about setting them up with a house and income and a college fund for the kid.

That will erase a little of the red off my ledger.

The red I can never get back? All the narcotic deaths and meth ODs from drugs I trafficked.

The drugs I helped to smuggle across the border.

The women I hurt.

I'll never be worthy of Katelyn. Never in a million years.

Once people realize I'm back in town, King will find out.

And I'll be dead.

But I'll die with Katelyn's mark on my flesh.

I'll die knowing I belong to someone—someone who loved me for me.

Rather, for the me I became. For the me I wish I could be forever.

Luke Johnson, no man and every man.

Except Luke Johnson doesn't exist.

My phone dings with a text.

I love it. It's beautiful. Please let me know where you are. I'm here in LA, as I've told you. My father woke up from the anesthesia and is fine. Biopsy results later.

She's here.

Which means I can't try to see her. To do so would put her in danger. To be anywhere near me in LA would put her in danger.

Why? Why did she come here?

Silly question, obviously. She came here for her father. She came here because she's a dutiful daughter and a wonderful person. A person I can never deserve.

I can't. I can't do this. I can't let her consume my thoughts. I can't give into the temptation to see her.

No. I just can't. I can't do anything that may put her in danger.

Except that I already know I will.

I'll see her.

I'll see her because I must. She's part of me now.

I'll find a way to keep her safe, even if I have to rely on my old man.

As much as I hate to admit it, my old man came through for me when I needed him after I got shot on the island.

He brokered the deal with the Feds, and he made me...

He made me invisible.

The decision to come back was mine, not his. Mine, because of Katelyn. Because I want to be worthy of her.

I've been back from the tattoo place for several hours now, and I had to bury my phone under a bunch of bedding to keep from texting Katelyn back.

I need to talk to my old man. I need to find out what he knows about that island, and why he was there. The last time we talked I kept mum about it. We thought, and we strategized.

I grab my phone from underneath the pillows. Nothing more from Katelyn, thank goodness. Really, I ought to block her. But I can't. That would hurt her so badly and I can't bear the thought of it.

I shove the phone in my pocket and head upstairs to the basement and then to the main floor.

My mother lights up when she sees me. "Are you going to join us for dinner, Lucy?"

"I suppose so. I need to talk to Dad. Is he home?"

"He's in his office. Dinner will be served in about a half hour. I'll have Dina set you a place."

"That would be nice." The least I can do for my mother is

eat dinner with her as her son. She deserves a lot more than she ever got from me. I turn toward the office and then look over my shoulder. "What's Sandy up to these days?"

"She's still trying to break into acting," Mom says. "She lives in an apartment near Hollywood."

My gorgeous sister always had the acting bug. She's beautiful and built but unfortunately doesn't have a lot of acting talent. I tried using my underground connections to get her into the movies a couple years ago, but I didn't have any luck. She blew all the auditions.

"I'd like to see her," I say.

"I can invite her to dinner next week," Mom says.

I shake my head then, changing my mind. "No. Never mind."

I already put my brother in danger by going to his place of business. He was the only person I wanted tattooing me. The only person I could trust to keep his mouth shut.

"I'm going to see Dad," I say.

Mom nods and smiles. Then she comes to me, embraces me, and gives me a kiss on the cheek. "I love you, Lucy."

"I love you too, Mom."

My father's office is on the east wing of our manse. I knock on the door.

"Yeah?"

"It's me. Trey."

"Enter."

Classic Lucifer Junior. He never says come on in, or anything like that. It's simply a solemn *enter*.

I enter. He doesn't look up from us desk.

"Dad, I need to ask you a question."

"Sit."

I sit.

"What is it?" Still not looking up.

"I need to know...what you did on Derek Wolfe's island."

Yup, that got him. He finally looks up, and his eyes—a darker blue than mine—look anything but happy.

"What the hell are you talking about?"

I clear my throat. "We've been through this. I have it on solid authority that you were on that island." If you call Yellow Eyes Pollack solid authority. I'm not sure I do, but my father doesn't need to know that.

"That island doesn't exist."

"Not anymore. The Wolfe family—"

My father's fist comes down on his desk. I don't jerk. I'm used to this kind of display from him.

"That island doesn't exist," he says again, this time through clenched teeth.

"Yeah, I get it. No one is supposed to know about it. Or *was* supposed to know about it. Most of the guys who went there seem to have walked free." *Yourself included*. But I keep those last two words to myself.

"How do you even know about it?"

"You think I never heard things? Maybe you and I didn't run in the same circles, but I had access to a lot of information in my line of business as well."

"In the drug business?"

"You know what kind of money is in the drug business," I say.

He flattens his lips. For a moment I wonder if he's going to rise and come grab me by the shirt.

I've never been afraid of him. Not since I went through puberty. I'm younger and stronger than he is, and I can take him. Still, my father will put up a hell of a fight, so I'd rather settle this with words.

"Listen, Trey. Whatever you think you know...there's no truth in it."

"You're saying you never went to that island?"

He doesn't reply. Which I take as an affirmation of yes, he was on that island.

"I know all about the place, Dad. I know what you did to women there. Quite frankly, I'm disgusted."

"Disgusted? You ran drugs, Trey. You contributed to the opioid epidemic. You contributed to all the meth and cocaine and fentanyl coming through the border."

"I won't apologize to you. I'm working on righting my own wrongs. I may never be able to do it, and I accept that. But you? If you were on that island—and I have it on pretty damned good authority that you were—anything I did pales in comparison."

"Some of your old girlfriends might not agree with that," he says.

"Low blow, Dad. I never raped anyone."

"No, you just exerted so much control that your women wanted to run away from you."

"I'm not proud of who I used to be," I say. "I'm here because I want to try to make up for it."

"And you think that's possible?"

"No, I don't. I don't labor under any delusion that I can make up for everything I've done. But I can do what I can. What are *you* going to do?"

"Who says I did anything wrong?"

"If you were on that island—"

"What if I was? You can't prove a damned thing."

"That's where you're wrong, Dad. I *can* prove it."

30

KATELYN

Luke doesn't return my text, of course. I'm not sure why I'm surprised.

At least I know he hasn't forgotten me. He had my name tattooed on his shoulder. His right shoulder.

That means something, right?

I smile. He still loves me.

When I return to the guesthouse, Jed greets me with a panting tongue in a wagging tail.

He also greets me with a floor full of white stuffing from a pillow he chewed up. I suppose I should be happy it's only one.

"Bad dog." I point to the pillow.

His tail is still wagging.

I can't resist. I kneel and hug him to me. "It's okay. It's your first day alone in the house. I'm lucky you didn't do anything worse." I open the sliding back doors that lead into the fenced yard and let him out. Then I scope out the first floor for any accidents.

Other than a tiny puddle in the kitchen by the door, it's

clear. A puddle by the door just means he was trying to go out.

He's a full-grown dog, so he shouldn't have too many accidents. He's just not used to being inside during the day.

This will work out fine.

I will eventually go back to Manhattan, and I'll need to find my own place that allows dogs. Jed is my link to Luke, and even if he weren't, I've already fallen in love with the silly mongrel.

I don't know how long I'll be here. It depends on what my father's biopsy results show.

Is it horrible to almost wish they come out bad? Because that will keep me here longer, and Luke is here.

I wipe the thought from my mind. It is a horrid, horrid thought.

Once Jed is done doing his business, I bring him back in and secure his leash to his collar.

"Time for a walk," I say.

Jed does fairly well on a leash. We walk for about forty-five minutes around our upper-class neighborhood. When both Jed and I have had enough, we return to the guesthouse.

A brown package sits on the stoop. There's no address on it. It says simply *Katelyn*.

My heart races. Is it from Luke? He could easily find me. He knows my last name.

"Looks like we got a surprise, baby," I say to Jed as I unlock the door.

I unleash Jed, and he scrambles inside heading straight for the kitchen where his water bowl is. I smile. He's already right at home here.

"I guess we should take you to the vet," I say. "I'll try to find an appointment for tomorrow. We need to make sure you get some shots and check out your health."

I turned my attention to the package. It's not big—about the size of a shoebox. It's wrapped in brown paper and secured with clear packing tape. I take it into the kitchen where Jed is still drinking, and I grab a serrated knife out of the utensil drawer. Carefully, I cut the packing tape and unwrap the brown wrapping.

Indeed, it is a shoebox. A Nike box. Strange, but he probably just used whatever box he had.

I open it and—

"Oh my God!" My heart thuds.

It's a timer. For a moment I imagine it's a bomb, but it appears to be only a timer.

It's set.

For two hours.

"I don't understand," I say out loud.

My skin prickles, and my heart continues to pound.

This isn't from Luke.

I need to call the cops. Maybe there are fingerprints on it.

"Thank you for calling 911," a dispatcher says, "what is your emergency?"

"A package was delivered to my home. It contains only a timer set for two hours."

"Ma'am, is the timer attached to anything?"

"No, it doesn't appear to be."

"Ma'am, leave your home. Someone will be there as soon as possible."

My heart races as I leash Jed again, leaving the package with the timer on the counter. Jed and I run to the main house.

"Mom," I yell after Casey opens the door for me. "We need to get out of here."

"Your mother is upstairs in the tub," Casey says.

"Fine. You and the others get out of the house. There's a…"

"What, miss?"

"There might be a bomb in the guesthouse. I don't think it's a bomb, but we have to—"

Casey's eyes widen. "The guesthouse is yards away, but we should get out of here."

"That's what I'm telling you. I have to get my mother." I hand Jed's leash to Casey. "Protect him. Please."

Casey nods as he leaves the house, yelling to the housekeeper.

I run up the stairs. I don't bother knocking on my mother's bedroom door or bathroom door. She's in the tub, lounging in a bubble bath.

"Mom!"

Her eyes pop open. "Katelyn, I'm in the tub."

"I know. Get out. Dry off and get some clothes on quickly. We need to get out of the house."

"What are you talking about?"

"There might be a bomb in the guesthouse. I don't think there is, but—"

She scrambles out of the tub and nearly slips on the floor. "What bomb?"

"Yes, a bomb. Someone delivered a timer to me. I don't think it's attached to anything, but the 911 dispatcher told me to get out of the house just in case. They're sending someone over to check it out."

"In the guesthouse?"

"Yes, the guesthouse. Come on. Let's go."

"The guesthouse is far enough away from the—"

Then a deafening sound.

An explosion.

Oh. My. God.

Oh my God.

OhmyGod.

My mother grabs me. "Are you all right?"

"Yes. Yes. Yes." My body is numb, as if it's not my own.

"Who would want to harm you, Katelyn?"

"I don't know. I don't know. I don't know."

My mind is a haze.

"Katelyn, my God. The guesthouse."

"I... I... I..."

"Your dog. Where is your dog?"

"My dog... Casey... Casey has the dog."

"Thank goodness. I know I gave you a lot of flack about him, but I wouldn't want anything to happen to an animal."

"Jed. Jed. Jed."

"Katelyn, snap out of it!" My mother pulls away from me, shakes me.

My clothes are wet now. My mom was wet when she grabbed onto me. She takes a towel and wraps it around herself. "Baby," she says, "I'm going to get dressed now. Are you all right?"

I don't reply.

I'm not sure if I'm all right.

Something terrible is happening. Something terrible, terrible, terrible.

Is it because of me? Is it because of that horrid thought I had about my father's biopsy?

"I'm..."

My mother takes my hand and leads me out of her bathroom and into her bedroom. She helps me sit down on the edge of her bed. "I'm going to get dressed now. Sit there. Sit tight."

Sirens in the distance. Blaring, blaring, blaring.

My mother puts on panties and a bra. I watch her, though I seem to see through her. Once she's dressed, she holds out a hand to me. "Baby, come on. The sirens are coming. The police are coming. Probably the fire engines too."

Fire engines? Of course. There was an explosion. There's probably a fire.

My suitcase. My personal belongings are in there.

But at least Jed is safe.

Jed...

Suddenly I want my furry companion more than ever. I don't know where Luke is, but at least I have his dog.

I follow my mother down the stairs to the first floor. Casey and the others have come back inside, and Jed rushes to me.

"Thank God you're all right," I say in a monotone.

"Casey," Mom says, "what's going on?"

"From what I can see," Casey says, "there's a small fire at the guesthouse. The fire engines are—"

The blaring gets so loud I can hardly stand it. Poor Jed is freaking out, running across the living room and back. Sirens must hurt his ears.

"I think they're here," Casey says.

"All right. Katelyn, you stay here with Casey. I'm going to go to the guesthouse and see what's what."

"Mom, no. Don't leave me."

"Someone has to take care of the situation. Your father's in the hospital. I'm all there is."

Is this truly my mother? Showing strength like this? My

mother who begged me to come home because my father was having a biopsy on a tumor that's most likely benign?

I see her through new eyes now.

My strength. I need to find my strength once more.

I inhale. "I'm coming with you, Mom."

"Are you sure?"

I nod. And then I swallow the lump in my throat. "I apologize. I'm sorry I went kind of catatonic on you. This probably has something to do with me."

"Who would want to harm you?"

"Probably a lot of people. Remember, I was held captive on that island for ten years."

My mom's jaw drops open. "But Katelyn, that wasn't your fault."

"I know, Mom. I know."

"Why would you have any enemies?"

"The men. I mean, I didn't know any of their names, but I gave information to the authorities."

"Those men all deserve to die."

"They're not all in prison, Mom."

She gasps. "They're not?"

"No," I say, my mind finally clearing. "In fact, I ran into one. In Manhattan."

31

LUKE

"So that's what you've got, huh?" Dad says. "Some derelict named Pollack said I was there?"

"Why would he lie to me?"

"Oh, I don't know. To cast your old man in a bad light?"

"He told me you were there before he knew who I was."

"If I had been there, on that island, do you think I would've been able to get the deal I got for you with the Feds?"

"Dad, I have no fucking clue. I don't presume to know how this all works. But I do know this. I had information that the Feds wanted, and I gave it to them. You had money. They also got a hell of a lot of my money."

"They *confiscated* your money, Trey. Because your money was made illegally."

"I made half a billion dollars doing what I did," I say. "I'm not proud of it, but the Feds took that money, so they're not hurting."

"Trey—"

"Just be honest with me for once, Dad. Please. Were you on that island?"

He doesn't reply.

"Look, I'm sure you got some kind of deal with the Feds. For God's sake, don't lie to me. Were you on the fucking island?"

After another eternity of silence, he finally nods. "I was there, Trey."

"Damn you." I shake my head.

"I didn't harm anyone."

"Oh?"

"Not everyone who went there hurt those women."

"Then what the fuck were you doing there?"

Silence again as he pauses. "I can't tell you."

I shake my head and scoff. "Just as I thought."

"No, you don't understand. I can't tell you. I'm under a nondisclosure agreement."

"With whom? Derek Wolfe? He's dead, so it no longer applies."

"Of course not with Derek Wolfe. I couldn't stand the bastard."

"With whom, then?"

"If I told you, I would break my agreement. Surely, son, after all the criminal activity you've been involved in, you understand the significance of a nondisclosure agreement."

Low blow, Dad. I don't say this, of course, because he's right. I *was* involved in criminal activity. I regret every minute of it...except for the one thing it led me to.

Katelyn.

If I had to be a drug kingpin, if I had to be King's right-hand man in order to meet Katelyn, then it was all worth it.

It's even worth my death. Even if I never see her again, I at least remember what it felt like to truly love and be loved in return.

"All right, Dad," I say. "Tell me what you *can,* then."

"I have, Trey."

I inhale and let out a breath slowly. He's not going to budge on this. I know my old man. He's a man of his word if nothing else.

"All I can tell you," he goes on, "is that I never harmed anyone while I was there."

I hope to God my father's definition of harm is the same as mine. "If you can't tell me anything else, why did you admit that you were there?"

"Because I *was* there, Trey. That's not a secret. You can find my name on any of the flight manifests."

"I see."

"If I had hurt anyone, do you think I would be walking around as a free man?"

"They're all free, Dad. All except that poor sap of a prince from Cordova."

"The principality of Cordova has different laws than the United States."

"Yeah, the US lets criminals go free for information."

"You really want to go there, Trey? It's because of the system here in our country that you're a free man as well."

I flatten my lips into a line. My father is not wrong, and I would do well to remember that.

"Why, then? So you can't tell me what you did on the island, why did you go?"

"Trey..." He gives me that "I'm your father and don't question me any further" look.

Though he gave up his right to claim fatherhood over me a long time ago.

"I'm not proud of everything I've done in my life. I wasn't the greatest father to you and your brother and sister. I know that, and I own it. But there are a few things I'm good at."

"Yeah, making money."

Dad scoffs. "Are you kidding me? I never had to lift a finger to make a dime. Our money was made two generations before me."

I nod. I know all this.

"I don't do any of the real work for the company. Producing is what I do, but I'm hardly on the A-list."

I say nothing. He's right.

"But there *are* a few things I'm good at," he continues. "One of those things is, I found out recently, helping the federal government."

A canary. My father's a fucking canary. Hell, I guess the apple doesn't fall that far from the tree after all.

"That's all I'm going tell you, Trey. I shouldn't have said as much as I have. The subject has got to be closed at this point."

"I get it now," I say. "You wanted me to squeal. Because you're a squealer."

"I wouldn't exactly put it in those terms."

"Then what kind of terms would you put it in?"

"Helping law enforcement get justice, Trey. That is exactly how I'd put it."

All this time, I've been hating myself for being a fucking narc.

But I'll give it to my old man. He just helped me see myself in a brand-new light.

One difference, though. If what he tells me is true, he was more of a plant. He wasn't a canary who turned on his friends like I was.

Still, I did help save a lot of people from drugs.

Of course, I also put them in danger in the first place.

Oh, hell. It doesn't matter how much red I erase from my ledger. I'll always be the guy who squealed on his buddies. I'll always be the guy who got out of a lifetime sentence because he was willing to turn state's evidence.

And I'll always be the guy who did the crime in the first place.

Even if my ledger contains only black, I'll never be good enough for Katelyn Brooks.

"Son?" my dad says.

"What?"

"Why are you back here? I want the true answer now."

"Doesn't matter."

"It does matter. I helped broker a deal for you. A deal where you'd be safe and secure. The only thing you had to do was stay the hell out of LA. So what do you do? You come back here."

I stand straight, regard my father. I look a lot like him. At least, when my hair and eyes are the right color. My father is still a handsome and robust man, with only a little bit of silver streaking through his dark blond hair.

I sigh. "I came back to be a better man."

"You can be a good man anywhere."

I shake my head. "I came back to right the wrongs, but I realize now that I can't do that. Some things can never change. Some things can never be reversed."

"That's true," Dad says. "But—"

"No buts." I shake my head vehemently. "I created the mess I'm in. I'll have to deal with it."

"Trey...don't. It will kill your mother. It was bad enough that you had to leave town and tell her you'd never see her again. But now you come back? If you leave her again, it will destroy her this time."

I don't reply. How can I? The only way to truly erase the red from my ledger is to give my life to take down the entire organization. I will do it.

Because my life is worth nothing. As much as it pains me, Katelyn needs to move on. She deserves so much better.

We'll both move on...after I see her one last time.

32

KATELYN

After talking to detectives on the bomb squad for what seemed like hours—apparently what looked like a simple timer was in fact the bomb—Mom and I check into the Beverly Hills Hotel. I have to pay extra for Jed, of course, but I don't mind. My mom and dad have money. I don't like taking it, but after I was almost killed, it doesn't seem as bad.

I saw another side of my mother today. She cared for me, called me baby, gave me strength.

So unlike her.

I came back from an island after being gone for ten years —ten years where my parents thought I was dead—and I got nothing but coldness from her.

I don't get it. My mother is beyond comprehension.

"Don't you think it might be better to put the dog in a kennel for a few days?" Mom says.

Okay, normal Mom is back.

"I want him with me," I say. "It's not up for debate. Jed and I can have our own room."

"Yes, I think that might be best."

Good. So much for the mother who cares.

Once Jed and I are settled in our room, I decide to text Luke. If he thinks my life was in danger, maybe he'll return my text.

I write a quick text.

My mom and I are at the Beverly Hills Hotel. No news on my dad's biopsy yet. We had a little bit of a scare earlier. I'm okay. I love you.

I wait.

And then I wait some more.

Luke doesn't reply.

I pull up the photo of his new tattoo once more.

His only communication with me since he left Manhattan.

In my heart, I know it means everything. But I'm scared. Is it possible he's not communicating with me because he can't? But he was able to get a tattoo, and he was able to send me a photo of it.

So he's not in danger.

I breathe a sigh of relief, but still sadness overwhelms me. I miss him. I miss him so much. I lie on my bed in the hotel, Jed sleeping soundly beside me. I stroke his soft fur.

"It's just for the time being, boy," I say. "We'll get through it. Together."

I lie down on the bed and snuggle with Jed, floating in and out of a light sleep. I don't know how long has passed when—

I jerk at the sound of a knock on the door.

Jed's ears perk up, and he lets out a quick bark.

I'm upright in a flash, my heart pounding. I didn't order room service. I draw in a deep breath and try to relax. It's probably just my mother. Perhaps she got the biopsy results.

I look through the peephole.

"Luke!" I throw the door open.

He stands there, wearing shorts and a tank. His tattoo...is gone. I fall into his arms.

"Baby, baby," he murmurs against my hair. "My God, Katelyn."

Sobs choke out of me, and I bury my nose in his shoulder —the right one, where he marked himself with my name.

He strokes my hair as he walks into the room, nudging me backward. Jed pounces around his legs.

Finally, after an eternity, I'm able to let go of him.

"Is that Jed?" he asks, kneeling.

I nod. "I brought him with me. I know it's silly, but he seemed like a link to you."

He rises and meets my gaze. "I can't stay."

"Why?"

"I... I can't. I had to know you were all right. That text..."

"Someone sent a bomb to my house, Luke. Why? Why would anyone do that?"

33

LUKE

"A bomb? A fucking bomb?"

"I know. Why?" she asks. "It's got to be someone from the island. Maybe that guy Pollack."

God, the rage. I know this rage. I know it like you know an old friend—the kind of friend you don't wholly trust, but you stay with him because of a shared history, because of some misplaced loyalty. And this time, that old friend has resurfaced with one thought in mind—to betray you for good. The anger glissades over my flesh, poking through every barrier and invading each cell of my body.

The strength of its fury surprises even me, and like that old friend you can't trust, it threatens to cross me, to take me over...and I'm only a hair away from letting it happen.

I could kill with my bare hands. I could mutilate whoever is responsible for this.

For placing my Katelyn in such danger.

"Luke?"

"It's not him. It's not Pollack."

"How do you know? It could be."

It's not, but I can't tell her that Pollack is under house arrest, by me, in Manhattan. I don't dare tell her that he's obsessed with her. I can't tell her anything. I shouldn't even be here.

But that text...

She told me where she was, and I raced to the Beverly Hills Hotel.

"It's not Pollack, Katelyn. Trust me."

"Of course I trust you. It's one of the others, then. But why?"

Why? It's no one from that damned island. It's King or one of his minions. Someone found out. The tattoo. Someone's watching me.

Fuck it all! I should never have come back here. I should have known what this would lead to.

I can't stay. I shouldn't be here now. I was careful coming here, but I'm obviously being watched like a hawk.

I kiss Katelyn's lips. "I have to go."

"No. Please. Stay. I need you."

She's shaking. Shivering. Someone tried to kill her. And here I am, telling her I can't stay.

Damn. I've only made things worse for her.

She clings to me once more, as Jed finally settles down in a corner of the room.

"Please," she says against my neck.

I'm not made of stone—except for my cock at the moment. I'm weak. Fucking weak. I lower my mouth to hers and kiss her hard.

She responds and opens to me, gives herself to me in that kiss. It's harsh and passionate and full of need all at once.

And it's the perfect outlet for that untrustworthy rage.

I deepen the kiss, losing myself in Katelyn's sweetness, in her goodness.

I back her toward the bed...

Clothes. Too many clothes. I rip my mouth from hers and then rip the clothes from her body. When she's naked before me, her ruby lips parted, I devour her.

My lips are everywhere—on hers, tracing her jawline, her shoulders, her perfectly shaped breasts. They clasp around her hard nipple, licking and sucking.

Downward, downward... I kiss every part of her all the way to her toes.

My cock is as angry as I am, and it wants relief as I do. I crave it, and I find it here, with my Katelyn.

I undress myself at warp speed, and then I'm inside her, one with her, and I take what she freely gives. I fuck her hard and fast, and within seconds I'm releasing and taking her with me.

We cling together as we come in tandem, our bodies one and our souls entwined.

And that rage? That old untrustworthy friend?

It softens.

But as we come down...I hold onto that old friend.

I hold onto him because I still need him.

I need him to avenge Katelyn.

34

KATELYN

I jerk out of a dreamy sleep to a short yip from Jed.

"Luke?" I sit up in bed, look around the room. It's dark.

How long have I slept? It's clearly nighttime. And where's Luke?

Then a knock on the door. Another yip from Jed.

"Just a minute!" I'm still naked, so I scramble into my clothes as quickly as I can, walk to the door, and gaze through the peephole into the lighted hallway.

Looks like a bellhop.

I open the door. "Yeah?"

"I'm sorry," the bellhop says.

"For what?" I wrinkle my forehead.

Then a plunge of something into my neck. Jed barks. Jed jumps on the bellboy.

And everything goes black.

35

LUKE

"What is it, Trey?" my dad asks.

I'm back home, thinking only of Katelyn, reading and re-reading her text from earlier. I don't know how best to protect her, and I'm ready to admit I need help.

I asked Katelyn to get me an audience with Reid Wolfe, but she's here now. In LA. Reid Wolfe can't help either of us here.

This is on me.

"It's..." I hand my father the phone. "The reason I came back, Dad."

"A woman?"

"*The* woman."

"Trey, you've had issues with women in the past."

"I know that. And believe me, I've had enough therapy to realize what I did wrong. I can't even blame the alcohol, although that was certainly part of it. I was fucked up in the head. Fucked up because of the criminal activities I got into.

But in the end, it was me. All me. I can't blame you or anyone else."

"You were blaming me?"

"For a long time, yeah. I mean, sure, you made mistakes. I don't mean to throw it in your face. For a long time, that's all I wanted. To throw it in your face. Blame you and others and everyone for things that were my fault. For the decisions I made. Now I know that the only person responsible for the way my life is gone is me."

"That's called growing up."

"I suppose I should've done it a long time ago."

"We all grow up in our own way, son. Trust me. It took me longer than it took you."

Trey would throw this back in his face. Would remind him of all the mistakes he made when I was younger.

But I'm no longer Trey. I'm Luke.

For the first time, I see how much I owe my father. Not only did he give me life, he gave me what by anyone's standards would be an idyllic childhood. Sure, he made mistakes. He wasn't there for me a lot of the time when I needed him. He took my mother for granted and mistreated her.

Looking at him now, I can see past his mistakes. He came through for me when I truly needed him. After I got shot and I was faced with a lifetime in prison.

For decisions I made. Me, not him.

"Tell me about her," Dad says.

"She's perfect. I never thought I could feel this way about another human being. And it's different this time. I don't have any need to control her, to lock her away and keep her safe. In fact..."

"What?"

"She's *not* safe with me, Dad. I know that now. I can't have her. But she's the reason I'm back. I thought if I changed things, if I made up for what I did, I could be worthy of her. Truly deserve her. But I now know that's not possible."

"Anything is possible, son."

I shake my head. "Not this. I've thought about it and thought about it and thought about it. Becoming worthy of her can only end in one way."

"What way is that?"

"In my death."

My father rubs his temples. "Trey, I want you to get the hell out of here."

"You're kicking me out?"

"That's not what I mean. You need to go back to Manhattan. No, it's too late for that now. You need to leave the country. Take refuge somewhere. You must go. Your death would kill your mother."

My mother. I don't want to hurt her, but my death is the only way this goes away. The only way Katelyn is safe. The only fucking way.

"Dad, I did a lot of harm. There's more red on my ledger than I can ever erase."

"Stop trying, Trey. Think of someone besides yourself."

"I *am* thinking of someone besides myself. I'm thinking of everyone I harmed along the way. I might be able to take King down, but the only way I can do that ends in my death."

"Please. I don't want to lose a child. But I will survive. It's not me you need to think about, Trey. It's your mother."

"I don't want to hurt her. Hell, I don't want to hurt you. Sure, there was a time when I did. And because of that need for harming someone, I ended up harming more people than I could ever imagine by getting into the drug business. I realize I'm lucky to be alive, Dad. What is one life compared to the countless others that will be harmed if I *don't* take King down?"

"You tried. You gave it your best shot. You took some others down, and you got out of the business yourself. You're no longer harming people."

"You're right. But I haven't paid my dues."

"What dues? Don't you think I wish I could take back every horrible thing I've ever done in my life? Don't you think everyone thinks that way as well? We all make mistakes, Trey. And some mistakes we just can't ever fix."

"Taking King down will fix a lot of it."

"Not if it costs you your life."

I shake my head. I appreciate my father's words. I probably appreciate them more than I've ever appreciated anything he's said to me in my thirty-plus years.

But there's only one way to make up for what I've done. Only one way to be worthy of Katelyn *and* ensure her safety.

I've had a lot of time to think about it while sitting around in that bomb shelter.

"Her name is Katelyn?"

"Yes."

He eyes the tattoo on my shoulder. "Does it hurt?"

"Yeah. But not in the way you mean." I hardly felt the needle, but now? The damned thing is ripping my heart out of my body, cell by cell.

"It looks shiny."

"It's a clear bandage. I can take it off in a few days. I need to moisturize it every day for two months." Basic tattoo care that I know from a long time ago. I expect to be dead before two months are up, but at least Katelyn will be a part of me when I go.

Her name tattooed on my shoulder is all I want to take of

her life. I want her to live a long and happy life. God knows she deserves it after what she's been through.

She will find love again. How could she not? She's the perfect woman.

"You never tattooed a woman's name on yourself before," he says.

"I've never loved a woman like this before.

"Then *live*, Trey."

Dad grabs my forearm, something he's never done before, at least not in my recent memory. My father and I aren't touchers.

"Live," he continues. "If not for your mother, if not for me, for Katelyn. Live for Katelyn."

My father's touch burns me, but not in a scorching or hurting way.

For the first time in a long time, if ever, I feel parental love coming from him.

And in that moment, I wish I could grant his request.

But I can't.

"Dad, someday you'll understand."

"Damn it, Trey, I understand now! The problem isn't that I don't understand, it's that I do. Do you think I've never done anything that I regret?"

"You haven't done what I've done."

The shred of doubt in my father dissipates. In that moment, I know he never touched a woman on that damned island. He's telling me the truth.

"That may be true, but I've made a lot of mistakes as a parent. Don't you think if I had done better, you wouldn't have run off to King?"

"Don't blame yourself, Dad. I don't. Not anymore."

"You did at one time. You did, and it probably was my

fault. Partially. Sure, you were an adult. You made the decisions, but if I had made different decisions during your childhood, you wouldn't have made the ones you did."

"This isn't your fault. And it certainly isn't Mom's. It's mine. Only mine, and only I can fix it."

He opens his mouth, but I shrug free of his grasp and speak over him.

"We can go on and on in this conversation. We've already repeated ourselves. I *will* take King down."

"Then we'll think positive, I guess. This doesn't mean you have to die."

I nod. I suppose there's a minuscule chance I'll live through it. What harm is there in giving my old man a tiny bit of hope?

My phone dings with a text. It's most likely Katelyn. She woke up and wondered—

But when I look at the words, my heart takes a nosedive.

36

KATELYN

Pins are pressing into my skull.

That's all I feel. Just pins—tiny sharp pricks that are sinking into my head.

The bomb. The hotel. Jed.

Luke. Luke coming to my room, making love to me.

I must be in bed at the hotel. Everything's a hazy dream.

"You're all right," a voice says.

I jerk upward and open my eyes. Images are blurred in front of me. Who's in my hotel room? Where's my dog?

"It's okay. I'm going to protect you as best I can.

The voice. It's deep, but it's not the deep voice I want to hear.

And I'm not where I'm supposed to be.

"Who are you?"

Already my skin is an icicle. This can't be happening to me again. No. What are the odds?

"Where am I? This is the hotel, right?" The words. They're not true. Already I know.

"This isn't the hotel," the voice says. "Someone brought you here."

No. No, no, *no*.

This is not happening to me again. This *cannot* happen to me again.

Remember your strength, Katelyn. You got through ten years on that horrid island, you can get through whatever is going to happen to you now.

How I want to believe myself. But everything's blurry. I can't even see the person to whom the voice belongs. The voice that claims I'm going to be okay.

"Luke, I want Luke," I say, closing my eyes once more. I can't stand the blurred images anymore. I just want to close my eyes and escape from all of it.

"I'm working on a plan," the voice says.

"No." I squeeze my eyes shut, try to feel at home on the bed. The bed that's not the hotel bed. The bed where Jed is not lying next to me.

"What's your name?" the deep voice asks.

Katelyn. Tell him Katelyn. But for some reason, I can't. I can't form the words.

"Moonstone," finally comes from my lips.

"Moonstone?"

I squeeze my eyes shut and nod.

"Open your eyes. Look at me. Look at me and tell me that's really your name."

I shake my head, my eyes still squeezed shut, refusing to accept this new reality.

And it *is* new. Despite my refusal to accept it, in my heart I know I'm not in the hotel. I know this man is not Luke. I know my dog is not here.

Why? Why is this happening to me again?

"Listen," the voice says. "I will not hurt you. I will try to protect you. But I need to know who you are. Really."

I don't reply.

"Was Moonstone your Treasure Island name?"

My eyes pop open, almost as if they have a mind of their own.

Whoever this man is, he knows about the island.

Which means he's no friend of mine.

"You stay away from me," I say between clenched teeth. "I will *not* go through that again."

"No, no. I'm not one of them. But I know about the island. I work for the Wolfe family."

I jerk upward once more. Everything is still blurry. "You do not work for the Wolfe family. The Wolfe family would never take me and put me somewhere against my will."

"You're right, they wouldn't. I didn't do this. Neither did they. I've been taken against my will also."

For a split second, I wish I could see the guy's face. I wish I could look into his eyes and see more than just a blur, because if I could, maybe I could tell if he's lying.

"I can't see," I say.

"I'm sorry about that. Your vision will clear. I don't know what they gave you, but whatever it is has probably affected your eyes. Are you feeling okay otherwise?"

"No. I'm not feeling okay. Where the hell am I?"

"As far as I can tell, at some kind of safehouse."

"Safehouse? Does that mean I'm actually safe?"

"Unfortunately, no. Safehouses are places criminals use to hide out."

"I'm not a criminal."

"Neither am I. I'm trying to take down some criminals."

"But you just said you work for the Wolfe family."

"I do. This is personal."

"So you're not working for the Wolfes right now?"

"No. I'm trying to find the motherfucker who tried to kill my sister."

I lie back down, close my eyes. If this man were going to hurt me, he probably would've done it by now. I don't feel as if I've been violated in any way, although whatever they gave me could be masking those feelings. It's obviously doing a number on my head and on my vision.

"Listen, Moonstone."

I jerk upward once more. "That's not my name."

"I know it isn't. You didn't give me your real name."

Why did I tell him Moonstone? I hated being Moonstone.

Will Moonstone always be a part of me?

The thought scares me, and although I desperately want it not to be true, I already know that it is. Ten years of my life can't be erased in a moment. I'm not sure why I ever tried.

How I wish I were back in Manhattan now. In a session with Macy, maybe talking to Zee or to Aspen. Getting on with my life.

Why did I come here, anyway?

For Luke.

Sure, my father had been in a post-anesthesia coma post, but he turned out to be fine. He probably has his biopsy results by now, and he's probably found out that his liver tumor is benign.

And Jed...

I rescued that beautiful dog, brought him here, which was a pain in the butt, and he probably hated being in the luggage compartment, and now where is he? I promised him a good life.

What will happen to him?

If someone took me from my hotel room, is he still in my room? He's probably hungry, thirsty. He needs to go outside and do his business.

I certainly can't depend on my mother to take care of him.

I choke back a sob.

No, I will not cry. I will not go back to that place.

"You all right?" The blurred figure of the man comes closer to me.

"You stay away from me," I say. "I'm fine. Fine."

"You don't need to back away from me," he says. "I said I wouldn't hurt you, and I do *not* break promises."

"Tell me your name, then."

"My name is Antonio Moreno," he says, his voice a deep rumble. "But people call me Buck."

37

LUKE

We have your woman.

That's all the text says.

Those words scare me enough, but it's the emoji that really makes my blood run cold.

It's a spade, like the card suit.

King's calling card.

The king of spades.

In the ancient tradition, the card suit of spades represents nobility. King always considered himself a king, not just a name.

The rage. My old untrustworthy friend.

It snakes along my spine like a cobra ready to strike.

Damn it, Trey, you're smarter than this.

I hear the words in my old man's voice.

I need his help. This isn't just about me anymore—about me and my worth and whether I deserve Katelyn.

No. Now it's about Katelyn herself. About the safety of the woman I love.

First, they sent a bomb. Now they've taken her.

All because of me.

I swallow the rage, gulp hard against it, because I need to be able to think clearly. All that matters now is Katelyn.

They haven't harmed her.

Her safety is at least guaranteed. They know I won't come if it's not.

Why did they have to bring Katelyn into it? Why didn't they just come and take me? My life is nothing without Katelyn.

But that's the point.

I worked with King long enough to know his MO.

He doesn't bother harming people for no reason. He doesn't bother taking people for no reason. He breaks a few legs when he needs to, but he keeps it business.

Families are off-limits. Loved ones are off-limits.

Which means this isn't business to him.

This is personal.

I'm not surprised. I knew it would be.

I knew I wouldn't get out of this alive.

But Katelyn… My sweet and innocent Katelyn.

There's only one thing for me to do.

Trade myself for Katelyn.

King doesn't want to find me. He wants me to go to him.

And he found the one thing that will get me there.

I text him back.

What do you want?

Your fucking head on a platter, Lucifer Raven.

Oh my God.

I've heard those words before, spoken to me but not texted.

Pollack. When he assaulted me at the bus station in Manhattan.

Fucking Pollack.

In cahoots with King.

Which explains how he knew my street name but not my actual identity. He knew only what King wanted him to know. How did King find Pollack? Is King still helping him? If so, then Pollack isn't staying at his studio.

Doesn't matter. None of it. All that matters now is protecting Katelyn.

Damn it.

You're smarter than this, Trey.

My old man's voice again.

I could go to him. I could get his help.

But I need to leave him out of this. He's done enough, all he can to ensure my safety. I can't drag him into this. He needs to take care of my mother, my brother, and my sister.

This is all on me.

You can have me, I text back. *My life for hers.*

You're not in any situation to make bargains, he texts back.

Anything. I'll do anything.

Yeah, you will. I'll be sending instructions. You will do exactly as I say.

I don't bother texting back.

He knows I'll do it.

He knows how important Katelyn is to me.

Now, more than ever, I'm ready to give my life. Ready to give my life for the woman I love.

I already knew I was a dead man.

Now? The only difference is I'm happy to be heading to my death. Happy...because it means Katelyn will survive.

38

KATELYN

Buck. The name sounds slightly familiar, but I can't place it. My head is still a mess. I feel like my skull is sitting on a bed of nails.

"Why are you here?" I ask.

"I made an error in tactical judgment," he says.

"What kind of an error?"

He doesn't respond right away. Just as well. I'm not sure I'm capable of understanding any error in any kind of tactical thing with my mind still in a haze.

"You see," he says finally, "I underestimated the power of the organization I'm dealing with. And I shouldn't have."

"Organization?"

"Yeah. We're being held by one of the most powerful drug organizations in LA."

"Drug organization?"

"Yeah. Whatever you did to get here, I'm sorry."

"You said..." What did he say actually? "You said you were looking for the person who tried to kill your sister?"

"Yeah. I shot the motherfucker, but he somehow managed to disappear. I thought he must be in prison, but he's not."

"Wait. What?"

"It's a long story. He followed my sister to some island, tried to take her back with him, and I shot him. I shot him while he had a knife to her throat."

Wait. I can't wrap my head around what I'm hearing. "I don't understand. What happened?"

"My sister. I shot him while he had a knife to her throat."

"You must be some shot."

"I learned from the best."

"Are you some kind of sniper?"

"Yeah. I was a Navy SEAL."

I swallow hard. "Your sister is lucky to have you."

"Not lucky enough. I should've kept it from happening from the beginning."

"I assume your sister was an adult at the time?"

"Yeah, but that's no excuse for me."

"What makes you think you could've stopped her?"

That actually gets a chuckle out of him. A freaking chuckle, when we're locked in here, my vision still compromised, and my head still swimming. And the pins in my skull are still tapping into me like sharp needles.

"I don't see anything funny about this."

"It's not funny. It's just... That's Emily. No one tells her anything."

"If she's an adult, that's normal."

"You're right. I couldn't have stopped her. And she managed to get away from the guy. That's how strong she is. He found her. He found her in the place where I took her to be safe. So I screwed up. I couldn't protect her."

"Where is she now?"

"She's..."

"Yeah?"

"She's fine. She's still on the island. Has a new guy. Has a job."

"Then why are you going after this guy?"

"Because he's a fucking menace to society and I want him to pay."

"Maybe he *is* paying."

"If he were paying, he'd be in fucking prison. But there's no record. I can't get any information out of anyone."

"Maybe he's dead."

"Then there'd be a death certificate. There isn't one. He just vanished into thin air. He was at a hospital, with the wound to his shoulder—"

"His shoulder?"

"Yeah. His shoulder. It's where I shot the fucker, remember?"

Luke had a scar on his shoulder. Where he got shot.

Luke. Where is Luke? Why hasn't he contacted me?

My phone is gone. I can't contact him now.

"I'm hungry."

"How long have you been here?"

"You tell me. You were apparently here when I woke up."

"They just put me in here with you. Just a little while before you woke up."

"What day is it?"

"I don't know. Friday, I think."

I open my mouth to speak but he talks over me.

"Maybe Thursday."

Monday was my first day on the job with the Wolfes. Then I left the next morning, which was Tuesday.

The explosion was Wednesday.

Okay, so Thursday makes sense.

"Why did they put you in here with me?"

"I don't know. But I promise you I won't harm you."

"Oh my God. They want you to hurt me?"

"They're probably thinking something will happen between us. Or they may try to force me to hurt you. I promise you that I won't."

My blood runs cold once more. Who are these people? And what do they want with me? I don't know anyone.

Except the Wolfes.

And apparently Buck works for the Wolfes as well.

"This must have something to do with the Wolfes," I say.

"Why would you think that?"

"Because that's the only thing you and I have in common."

He doesn't respond at first.

"I suppose you're right," he says finally, "but I'm not working for the Wolfes right now. And I don't know why this drug organization would have any ties to the Wolfes at all."

"But that's the only tie you and I have."

"So it would seem."

"What's that supposed to mean?"

"It means," he says, "that there must be some other reason you're here."

I drop my jaw. Why would some drug cartel have any interest in me?

My vision is clearing a bit. Finally.

I can see Buck. He's tall and muscular, wearing jeans, army boots, and a long-sleeved T-shirt. His hair is long and dark, covering his ears, and his eyes are brown.

A good-looking man, definitely Navy SEAL material.

"I don't know," he replies. "But there's some reason you're here. These guys don't take people for no reason."

"Maybe they do. Maybe they saw me and—"

"No. They don't. You're here for a reason, but I don't know what it could be."

"You really don't think it's the Wolfes."

"Absolutely not. I don't know why this organization would have any interest in the Wolfe family."

"Then why?" I asked. "Why me?"

"Tell me. Tell me everything you've done in the last week or two. There's got to be some connection."

"I just came to LA because my father had a liver biopsy."

"What's your name?" he asks. "Your real name."

I swallow. "Katelyn. Katelyn Mary Brooks."

"Your parents' names?"

"James and Farrah Brooks."

"Doesn't ring a bell."

"I told you. There's nothing. Nothing at all."

"What else have you done the last couple weeks?"

"I just returned from the island—the retreat center—to Manhattan. And I was working for the Wolfes. Well, starting. I didn't get very far."

"The island. Billionaire Island.

"Billionaire Island?"

"It's kind of the new name for Wolfe Island. What people are calling it."

"Well, it was Wolfe Island, yeah. That's where they built the retreat center. For the other women like me."

"So you just came to Manhattan, and you were starting work for the Wolfes. What else?"

"Well...I did meet a man."

"Oh?"

"Yeah. His name is Luke. Luke Johnson."

"Tell me about Luke Johnson."

"He's a waiter. At a restaurant called The Glass House. Except he left. He's here in LA now. He said he had to take care of some things."

"What kind of things?"

"I don't know. He didn't tell me."

"I see."

"What do you mean you see? You can't possibly think Luke has something to do with this."

"I don't know for sure, but the vagueness of your statement has me concerned."

"Vagueness?"

"Yes. When was the last time he contacted you?"

"He... He came to my hotel room. I fell asleep, and when I woke up, he was gone."

Buck meets my gaze. "Houston, I think we have a problem."

39

LUKE

I've been in situations where I have to keep my cool. I'm good at it. It's the reason I was successful for as long as I was in the organization. It's the reason why King trusted me to be his right-hand man.

It's also the reason I thought I could get away with finding Emily and taking her from a private island with heavy security.

While I was in recovery, my therapist said he thought I had narcissistic tendencies. I fought him on this. But looking back, I see he was right.

Failing never entered my mind. That's why I was so good at what I did.

It ultimately led to my demise. When Emily's brother shot me on the island. And I was arrested.

Turns out that wasn't my demise. Turns out it saved me. It helped me bring down some master criminals, and it led me to Katelyn.

Funny. I used to have ice in my veins. I could get through anything. Take care of anything King asked of me.

Until now.

The ice in my veins? It's been replaced with boiling honey. That heartbeat I used to be able to control? No longer. My heart races for Katelyn. Fear. A new emotion for me.

I fear for her life.

And I'm willing to give mine for hers.

Definitely new.

Perhaps my life was easier before I was shot. Nothing used to bother me. I was cold. Totally coldhearted with regard to my work. Totally hot-blooded with regard to women. I yearned to control them. And I kidded myself. I told myself it was because I loved them, wanted to protect them.

It wasn't that at all.

I was a mess.

And now? I care so much. I care about Katelyn most of all, but I also care about my mother, my father, my brother and sister.

I care about my life.

I'll gladly give mine for Katelyn's, and I know that's what will ultimately happen.

But damn it, I want to live! For the first time, I want to fucking live. With Katelyn. I want to make a family. I want to be a father.

All those other women? I never had these desires.

But it will have to be enough to know Katelyn will live. That Katelyn will be a mother and wife to someone else. Someone else who will love her as much as I do.

Though I don't see how that will ever be possible.

My heart is beating out of my chest. And the rage—that flawed friend...

I need to do something. What?

Until I receive instructions via text, there's nothing I can do.

I used to know where all of King's safehouses were, but he's too smart to put Katelyn in one of them. Once I turned, King had to regroup.

And while word on the street was that he fled to Mexico, I always knew better.

As soon as I got here to LA, I felt him. I knew he was here.

I was right. He's here. He's out for blood.

And there's nothing I can do.

Nothing...until I hear from him.

I scroll back through all of the texts Katelyn sent me. How I wish I could go back in time and return each one of them. Or, better yet, go back to that hotel room and never leave her side. Tell her to her beautiful face what she means to me. How much I love her. And though I'll never be able to be with her, how much I wish things were different.

How she deserves everything good in life. Everything I can never give her. And that even in death, no one will love her as I do.

Why did she have to come to LA?

First thing I should do is check on her father. Although no one will give me any information. And that would just alarm her parents.

A run might take the edge off. But I can't. I can't do anything that may risk me not getting the instructions. If I'm running, I might not hear my phone.

"For God's sake," I say out loud. "I will kill you, King. I will fucking kill you for this."

My phone dings.

For a moment, I think he actually heard me. Actually heard me say I would kill him.

But it's a marketing text. I delete it and then hurl my phone across the room.

My old friend rage wins out again.

Not my best move, since I need the damned thing. I walk across the floor, pick it up, and see that it's still working.

Good.

I rake my fingers through my short brown hair.

If I live through this—which I won't—I can go back to my natural blond hair. It will take years to grow it out to where it was, but I don't give a rat's ass.

Blond, brown. What the hell difference does it all make?

What the hell difference does it all make?

King is doing this to me on purpose. Making me wait. He knows it's driving me slowly insane. Which is what he wants.

I've got to keep it together. I've got to keep it together for Katelyn.

Her safety depends on me.

Which means I cannot screw this up.

God, I want a drink. I want a drink so badly. A nice smoky bourbon that burns my throat. Just one sip. That's all I need to take the edge off.

Just one sip.

I walk. I walk toward my parents' liquor cabinet.

One step. Two steps. Then three and four steps.

Again and again, I step, until I'm standing right in front of the mahogany cabinet.

Inside is the best liquor money can buy. My old man is a scotch drinker, but he keeps a little bit of everything for any guests who may be here.

Inside will be the premium bourbon.

Just between this wooden door and me.

I crack open the door. Look inside.

All the bottles.
Just one.
Just one sip. It will help.
I need to be calm to get through this.
I pull the bottle off the shelf, and—
My phone dings with a text.

40

KATELYN

"What do you mean?" My heart beats rapidly against my chest.

"There's a reason you're here," Buck says. "I know these guys. They don't take people for no reason."

"Meaning..." I gulp.

"Meaning you're important to someone."

"I'm a no one. I'm not important to anyone."

"Except your waiter friend."

"But I told you. He's nobody. He's a waiter in Manhattan."

"Is he?"

"I..."

Is he? I don't know. I know very little about Luke. Except that I love him. I love him so very much.

"Listen," Buck says. "I don't want to scare you. That's the last thing I want. But I know you're here for a reason. Maybe it's not your boyfriend. Maybe it's someone else."

"I don't know anyone else. I've been gone for—"

"What about your parents?"

"My dad's a tech guy. We're well-off, but we're not billion-aires or anything."

"And there's no way your father would be involved in any kind of drug business?"

"No. I told you. My father's in the hospital."

"Anyone else?"

"Just the Wolfes. And..."

"And what?"

"Well...I ran into one of the guys from the island in Manhattan. He recognized me. His name is..." *Ice Man. His name is Ice Man*. "Pollack, I think."

"Okay. Now we may be getting somewhere."

"Okay."

"Tell me everything about this Pollack."

"It's... I don't like to talk about it. He was one of the guys who came to see me on the island."

"You don't need to go into detail. I just need to know if he may have any connection to this drug organization."

"He should be in prison, obviously."

"He probably turned evidence."

"Yeah. That's what Luke said."

"Luke. The boyfriend."

"Right."

"What does Luke look like, Katelyn?"

An interesting question. "He has brown hair and brown eyes."

Buck nods.

"Except...he doesn't."

Buck drops his mouth open. "What the hell do you mean?"

"He colors his hair and wears colored contacts. Appar-ently he's actually blond...with blue eyes."

Buck pushes his hair back from his forehead. "Blond with blue eyes? Is his hair long or short?"

"It's short. Why?"

"I guess he could cut it."

"What are you talking about?"

"In fact, of course he cut it. If he's hiding from King. Hiding from me. Hiding from everyone." Buck seems to be talking to himself now.

"Let me in. What are you talking about? You're scaring me." My words are ridiculous, of course. I'm already scared out of my mind.

"Just a theory, but I'm wondering if your waiter from Manhattan is the man I'm looking for."

"The man who hurt your sister? No, he can't be. Luke is kind and gentle." I curl my hands into fists on instinct. No way will I let this guy malign Luke's good name.

"Yeah, it's a long shot."

"Of course it is."

"But still... There's a reason you're here, Katelyn. And if Luke is who I'm looking for, that would explain it."

"Why? Why would that explain it?"

"Because the man I'm looking for is the son of a local producer from old money. His real name is Lucifer Charles Ashton the third, but his street name is Lucifer Raven."

My jaw drops.

"What?" Buck asks.

I have no words. All I can think about is that tattoo of the raven on Luke's left arm and shoulder. Black and red with fire shooting from its wings.

It's a remnant of something I'd rather forget.

Luke's words.

No. It can't be.

My Luke would never harm anyone. My Luke is a good man. The *best* man. He feeds stray dogs.

He loves me. He wasn't lying about that. Words are just words, but I felt it. I felt his love for me.

"Katelyn..."

I shake my head. "No. Absolutely not. Luke is not the man you're looking for."

"He may not be. But you're here for a reason, like I've said. I have to consider the possibility."

"Tell me, then. Tell me all about this Lucifer Raven."

"You'd know him if you saw him. Blond and blue eyes like you said, and he has a tattoo," Buck says. "On his left arm and shoulder."

My stomach turns. Acid crawls up my throat, and I retch.

It's dry heaves. I'm not sure when I last ate, and luckily nothing comes up, but I retch. It hurts my throat, and I double over with cramps.

Buck rushes toward me, helps me to a bathroom that I didn't even know was there.

Then I'm in front of a toilet, still dry heaving.

"It's okay," Buck says softly. "Let it out. Let it all out."

But nothing comes out.

Empty. I'm empty.

And I fear I'll never be filled again.

41

LUKE

Go to the Beverly Hills Hotel. A car will come for you.

Thank God. At least now there's something I can do. I race out of the house, ready to go when—

"Lucy?"

Shit. My mother.

"Yeah, Mom?"

"Your sister is coming for dinner. Your brother also."

"All right, Mom."

"They're both looking forward to seeing you."

"I already saw Bas."

"Yes, he mentioned that."

"Mom, I've got to go."

"Dinner's at seven o'clock sharp," she says. "Don't be late."

"Right." Then I walk toward her, give her a kiss on her cheek. "I love you, Mom."

She lifts her eyebrows. "I love you too, Lucy."

She's surprised. I can't remember the last time I told anyone in my family I love them. But I do, especially my mother.

She's the one who always believed in me.

As I look at her beautiful face, her blue eyes so much like my own, I realize this is the last time I'll see her.

Ever.

"See you at dinner," she says with a smile. "And Lucy?"

"Yeah?"

"It's so good to have you home. It's just so...good."

I nod.

Losing me will kill my mother, as my father says.

I wish things were different. I wish I could go back ten years and make different decisions.

But I can't, and it has all led me to this.

"Mom, I want you to do something for me."

"Of course, Lucy. Anything."

"There's a woman. Her name is Katelyn Brooks. Her parents live here in LA somewhere. Her father's in the hospital, something with his liver. He's waiting for biopsy. She and her mother are at the Beverly Hills Hotel."

"Okay. What about her?"

"She deserves the best. Could you do something for me?"

"I can try."

"Take care of her. Find her and take care of her. Make sure she has the best of everything."

"Lucy, I—"

"Love you, Mom." I kiss her cheek again. "See you at dinner."

The words are acidic on my tongue. They're a lie, but I need to give my mother this. I need to give her an afternoon free from worry.

The worry will come soon enough.

An hour later, after grueling traffic, I'm waiting outside the Beverly Hills Hotel.

Car after car, limo after limo, and none are for me. Until—

A silver Mustang drives up. A man dressed in black gets out of the car and meets my gaze.

"Luke Johnson?"

"Yes."

"Get in the car."

I WAS INSTRUCTED to lie down in the back seat. Honestly, I'm surprised he didn't drug me and blindfold me, but I guess they know how important Katelyn is to me.

Obviously they do, or they wouldn't have taken her.

We drive for a while, over an hour. I have no idea where we're going. I don't dare try to look. Any disobedience and they may harm Katelyn.

I want to ask questions as well, but I don't.

Whoever this guy is, he has his instructions, and one of them is undoubtedly not to answer any questions from me.

I know how these things go.

Hell, I used to be in the driver's seat. This was my job when I was new in the organization. I was the person who showed up as a driver, who took people where they were supposed to end up.

And a lot of them never saw the light of day again.

No, I never pulled the triggers—not once—but I contributed to many deaths.

Most of them were more people like me—people who fled the organization or at least tried to.

How did I ever think I could deserve Katelyn? How did I ever think I might possibly be worthy?

I'll take death by a thousand paper cuts—I'll take death in the most heinous, horrid, torturous way possible—to save her life.

To make sure she has the life she deserves.

Finally, the car pulls into a driveway and stops.

"Get up," the driver says.

I rise into a sitting position.

I don't recognize the place, which of course I don't expect to.

"What now?" I ask.

"That's not for me to say."

When he opens the door, I get out. I stand on my own two feet. Determination courses through me. My old friend rage appears, and I attempt to keep him in check.

Whatever King makes me do, I'll do it.

Anything for Katelyn.

A house. An old country farmhouse. Seemingly in the middle of nowhere, yet I can see the LA skyline through the smog on the horizon.

We're not overly far from the city.

This is a safehouse. Already I know this. Already I know King is here.

I feel him. Insects crawling up the back of my neck. That's King.

And Katelyn.

Meandering alongside the insects is warmth, love.

Katelyn is in this house.

And so far she hasn't been harmed.

It's my job to make sure it stays that way.

"Follow me."

I obey the driver. It's not like I have any other choice. We go inside the house, and of course it's empty. Or so it appears to be.

"Where's King?"

I don't expect an answer, and I don't particularly want one.

The driver takes me into the kitchen and nods toward a seat at the table. "Sit down."

I drop my ass to the chair.

The driver opens the refrigerator and pulls out a plate and a glass. He sets both in front of me. "Eat."

It's a roast beef sandwich with some kind of cheese and a glass of water.

"I'm not hungry."

"I didn't ask if you are hungry. Eat."

Maybe the sandwich is laced with something. But if he wanted to drug me, he would've done it before now. I pick up the sandwich and take a bite. Tastes kind of like dirt.

I try to swallow my bite, but it forms a firm lump in my throat. I take a drink of the water to dislodge it.

Then I take another bite. A drink of water. I continue this until the sandwich is gone.

So far I don't feel anything, though any drugs ingested orally will take a while to get into my bloodstream.

"You need to use the bathroom?" the driver asks.

"Yeah." I don't, but I want to look at the lay of the land as well as I can.

"Follow me."

I rise and follow him down the hallway to a door. "Don't take too long. I'll be waiting."

Great. Not that I expected anything less. He's no doubt been instructed by King to keep both eyes on me at all times. Part of me is surprised he doesn't watch me take a piss.

But he doesn't, and for that I'm grateful. There's little to be grateful for, but at least I have this, a modicum of privacy and modesty.

What I'm most grateful for right now is my knowledge— my knowledge of King and his MO, which tells me Katelyn hasn't been harmed.

No, King will save that. If I don't cooperate to his satisfaction, he will begin harming Katelyn. He'll probably make me watch.

That way, he'll get me to do whatever he wants.

He knows this, and so do I.

Yes, I'm well versed in his MO.

I manage to squeeze out a few drops of piss and flush the toilet to make it look good. While the toilet is flushing, I open the mirrored cabinet above the sink. Nothing in there except a pack of antibacterial wipes.

Then I open the cupboards below the sink. Nothing again.

Then, just for kicks, I turn on the water to wash my hands, and while it's running, I lift the lid to the toilet tank.

I don't know what I'm expecting to find. Toilet hooch? A nail file? Something as small as a paperclip?

I don't find any of those things, but I do find something.

Something that could very well help me.

42

KATELYN

The violent heaves finally stop, but my stomach is cramped so badly I can't seem to move. Buck helps me up, but still I'm hunched over. He walks me out of the small bathroom and back into the room and to the bed where I first woke up.

"Lie down," he says.

I obey, and lying flat helps the cramping a bit.

"Easy," he says. "Everything will be okay."

I don't reply.

I don't reply because it's a lie. Everything will *not* be okay. Everything is so far from okay. Here I am, having been taken against my will once more.

It wasn't enough that someone tried to kill me earlier. With the bomb.

When that didn't work, I guess they decided to take me instead. But something doesn't jibe. If they wanted me dead, why would they bother taking me and bringing me here?

"I don't understand," I say.

"Understand what?" Buck asks.

"Someone sent a bomb to my house yesterday. Or the day before. I have no idea."

"What?"

"I know. Crazy. It was a package left on the doorstep of the guesthouse behind my parents' house where I'm staying. I opened it, and as soon as I figured out what it was, I left the house. The bomb squad came, but it blew up anyway. I don't even know the extent of the damage. But my mom and my dog and I got out. We were staying at the Beverly Hills Hotel, and then—" I shake my head. "Somehow I ended up here."

"I admit that doesn't make a lot of sense. Are you sure it was a bomb?"

"Well, something blew up."

He doesn't reply.

"Whoever sent the bomb clearly wanted me dead, right? But if that's the case, why am I not dead? Not that I want to be dead. But..."

"The bomb was a decoy, I bet. How did you know to get out of the house?"

"The timer was set for two hours, so you can bet I ran out of there."

"Yup, a decoy. It was a scare tactic. I hate to tell you this, Katelyn, but your boyfriend may very well be behind this."

I close my eyes, shake my head. "No. He wouldn't do this. He loves me."

"Lucifer Raven doesn't know the meaning of the word love," Buck says. "Believe me. I know."

"Maybe he's changed. Did you know he's a recovering alcoholic?"

"No, I didn't."

"Was he a big drinker?"

"Come to think of it," Buck says, "I'm not sure I ever saw

him without a drink in his hand. But he never seemed to be drunk."

"Oh?"

"But that could mean that he was just so tolerant of the alcohol that it didn't make him drunk in the normal sense."

"Isn't that called a functioning alcoholic?" I ask.

"I don't know anything about alcoholism, thank God. But he was a fucked-up mess, Katelyn. He abused my sister. Kept her locked up. He even…"

"What?"

"I don't want to have to tell you this. I really don't want to have to destroy the image that you have in your head. But he hit my sister. More than once."

My hands fly to my mouth.

No. Not Luke. Luke would never strike a woman. He's a gentle and caring man.

"I see that surprises you." Buck rakes his fingers through his hair.

"I just can't believe it. There must be two different people. My Luke is not your Lucifer Raven."

"Somehow I doubt that two people have that exact same tattoo."

"How do we know it's the same? Do you have a picture of it?"

"As a matter fact, I do. Of course it's on my phone, which I don't have on me at the moment."

"Can you draw it?"

"Maybe a crude replica," he says, "but I doubt there's a pen and paper in this room."

"Why wouldn't there be?"

"Because a pen can be used as a weapon. Anything with a point can."

"Right." I should know that. We weren't allowed to have pens in the dorm on the island.

We weren't allowed to have anything sharp.

I never had anything sharp...but I had something I shouldn't. That porcelain plate—that plate that I could have broken and used as a weapon. The plate I hid under my mattress.

A figurative punch to my already cramped gut.

I remember that plate.

And I remember what it cost me.

DIAMOND COMES for me early one morning.

"Katelyn." She rouses me out of bed. "Katelyn, you need to get up. Now."

"Why what's going on?"

"Apparently you were hiding something under your mattress. One of the housekeepers found it."

My heart drops to my belly. The plate. "It's been there for... I don't know. Months?" I never really know what time it is around here, or what day for that matter.

"We can usually trust these people, but apparently someone new cleaned your room yesterday. Usually the housekeepers come to me, and I do my best to protect you girls. But this time..."

"This time...what?" I squeeze the back of my neck. Already goosebumps are forming all over my flesh. Fear. Unadulterated fear.

"What else can they do to me that they haven't already done?" I ask Diamond.

Later, I find out.

~

"THEN DESCRIBE IT," I say. "Describe the whole thing."

"I think I already did. I never actually saw it in its entirety. Emily had a picture. A photograph. She sent it to me. That's why I have it on my phone. But who knows what they did with my phone?"

"I don't have a photo, but I'll never forget it. It was...beautiful in its way. I'm not really into ink, but it worked on him."

"I see."

"He didn't show it to me for a while. He always wore long sleeves. In fact, the first time we ever—"

I gasp.

"What?"

"The first time we were...intimate. He wore a long-sleeved shirt."

"And you didn't think that was a little odd?"

"In retrospect, yes. But I had my own scars I was hiding as well."

"You poor thing."

"They're mostly on my back. I had it a lot easier than some of the women on the island."

"Sweetheart, none of you had it easy."

"You're right." I gulp. "And now that you mention it, yes, the fact that he wore long sleeves when we made love—" I clasp my hands to my mouth.

"It's okay. I hate the fact that he was anywhere near you, but if we're going to get through this, you have to be completely honest with me."

"Okay." I nod. "Yes, the long sleeves were weird. I suppose you think it's strange that I didn't really consider that at the time. But I... I never imagined feeling the way I felt when I was with him. He was so kind and gentle."

Buck's eyebrows rise.

"I mean it. I've never been with anyone as kind as Luke."

My words are ridiculous, of course. My experience with men was limited to high school and the island, so really I don't know anything.

"Black and red are the two main colors," I say, closing my eyes and visualizing Luke's left arm. "The first time I met him, at the restaurant, I noticed the black and red swirls on his left hand. He was wearing long sleeves, so I had no idea what they led to, but it was clear that they were the ending of something. I didn't recognize the design. I'm not really that well-versed in design. But I can say it looked more tribal than Celtic, if that makes any sense."

Buck nods. "Yes. That does make sense."

"Anyway, the tribal markings went up his forearm to his upper arm, where they turned into a Raven with red eyes and flames for wings. And then the tribal designs wrapped up around onto his left shoulder."

Buck nods. "Sounds a lot like Lucifer Raven's tattoo."

I can't cry. I want to, but I can't.

Does Luke even deserve my tears? I shed a lot for him when I thought he left me.

Turns out he came back.

Why? I still don't know exactly why all of this is happening.

"Tell me," I say to Buck. "Tell me everything you know about Lucifer Raven."

43

LUKE

I learned from the best. Career criminals who used everything at their disposal as a means for weapon or escape.

I have no desire to escape. Katelyn is here, and I can't help her if I can't get to her.

I'm not looking to escape. No, I'm looking for something I can use as a weapon.

I jerk at a pounding on the door. "Hurry it up in there. You're taking too long."

"I'm washing my hands, asshole."

I cringe. I probably shouldn't be name calling, but if the shoe fits...

Quickly I reach into the toilet tank and grab the half-dissolved tablet. It's toilet cleaner and deodorizer. Our housekeeper at home uses them in all our bathrooms.

It's made of some kind of disinfectant, and it will pack a wallop if I can get it in someone's eyes.

How? I have no idea. But it's a hell of lot better than nothing.

Do I really think I can beat King with a toilet cleaning tablet? Fuck it all. I suppose stranger things have happened.

Now, what to do with it. It's wet, so I wrap it in toilet paper as best I can and shove it into one of my front pockets.

And I hope like hell it doesn't seep through the toilet paper and give me away. At least it's blue and my jeans are blue. Maybe it'll just look like I pissed myself a little.

I turn off the water, making sure I leave a little of the tablet on my fingertips. If I can get near the driver's eyes, perhaps I can get him.

A paperclip would be better. A nail file. Tweezers. A razor blade would be great.

But all I have is a toilet cleaning tablet that looks like a large blue Alka-Seltzer.

I leave the bathroom and close the door.

"Took you long enough."

"Did you want me not to wash my hands?"

For a moment I fear he may actually want to see my hands. But he doesn't. Good. I don't need him to see the bit of dried tablet powder.

"Now what?" I say.

"What makes you think you can ask questions?"

"You just did." I'm being a smartass. Not my best move, but I've been on the other end of this so often that I'm used to being a smartass. "What's your name?"

"I think that's a question."

I say nothing more as I follow him back through the hallway to the kitchen.

"You need anything else to eat?"

"No."

"You may want to reconsider your answer. I don't know when I'll be able to offer you food again."

"In that case, sure."

He heads to a kitchen cupboard and pulls out a couple of granola bars. "Here."

"What am I supposed to do with these?"

"Hold onto them. Or put them in your pocket."

Pocket? I'm not putting anything that may be going into my mouth in the pocket with the half-dissolved toilet tablet.

"My pockets aren't big enough. I'll just hold onto them."

"Suit yourself."

He doesn't tell me to follow him, but I do. What else am I supposed to do?

"Where's King?" I ask.

"You keep thinking you can ask questions here."

"We both know why I'm here. We both know you have Katelyn. We both know King wants me dead."

"If we both know, why are you asking me so many questions?"

"Look, I don't care about myself. Do what you want to me. Make me suffer all kinds of horrible stuff. Just let her go."

"It's not up to me, dude."

Dude? Strange. I wonder if this guy could potentially be a friend.

"What are you doing here, man?" I ask.

"My job."

"Take it from someone who knows. You're going to live to regret this."

"That's not for you to say."

"Hey, we both know it's too late for me. But you can still get out."

"You don't know what you're talking about."

I chuckle at that. Seriously chuckle, even in my current circumstances. "Man, I'm the one guy who *does* know."

He doesn't reply. Why should he? He and I both know I speak the truth.

We head down a spiral staircase to what I assume is a basement. Still, I'm amazed I'm not blindfolded. Just further evidence that my fate is sealed. King and I both know I'm not getting out of here alive, so it doesn't really matter whether I know where I am and can describe what I've seen.

I follow the driver to a locked door. He opens it with a combination.

35742.

I learned a long time ago to memorize numbers quickly.

Even so, I know it won't matter. I won't be able to access the lock from inside the room. Still, I keep the numbers in my head. You never know when they might come in handy.

He shoves me through the door. "Wait here."

"For what?"

"That's all I know. I do as I'm told. Just like you do." The driver closes the door and clicks it locked.

As I suspected, there's no way to unlock it from the inside. Such a fire hazard. Of course that doesn't matter to King.

Oddly, there *is* a window well. No bars.

An escape route. One I won't use.

King knows this. He knows I won't go anywhere because he knows that I know he has Katelyn.

He's dangling these carrots in front of me, daring me.

I'm not that stupid—something he also knows.

In the room is a bed, a door leading to a toilet and sink, but no shower. Also a chair and a desk. Even a pen. Yup. He knows I won't try anything.

Or he's betting I might, and the first thing he'll check when he comes to get me is whether the pen is still sitting there.

So I don't touch the pen. I go into the bathroom, and to my surprise—or to my non-surprise—I find a nail file and a razor blade sitting right on the rim of the sink.

He's given me a means to try something on him or even to off myself with the blade.

As long as he has Katelyn, I won't do anything. Both he and I know this.

I'm not even slightly tempted.

But then I realize he's done something else as well. He's given me these means as a way to test me. He's going to test how loyal I am to Katelyn. How strong my feelings are for her.

I'm betting he thinks I'll choose myself in the end.

He thinks wrong.

Nothing to do now except wait. Though I do check the inside of the toilet tank. There's another tablet, this one even more dissolved than the first.

Makes me wonder if the tablets are there for a reason other than disinfecting toilets. Does he know I'll try to use it as a weapon?

Or are there tablets in every toilet, just as there are in my own home?

Could go either way, but I'm betting on the latter. I have to. I have to stick my faith in something. I have to believe I have some way of helping Katelyn.

I'm toast. No way will I get out of this alive. But I have to get *her* out before they harm her.

And they *will* harm her.

It's part of the way he plans to torture me.

A big part of me even believes I deserve the torture.

I'll take whatever he has to give.

But before I do that, I have to get Katelyn out of here.

She's here in this house. Somewhere.

And she's scared. She's so very scared.

I will get her out of here. Doesn't matter what happens to me at this point. I've accepted my fate.

But I have not yet accepted hers.

44

KATELYN

"He's a monster."

Buck's words cut through me like a dull knife. No, this isn't a clean cut. It's jagged and raw, leaving my insides open and sore.

He's a monster.

The words echo in my head in Buck's deep voice.

His tone is serious and his facial muscles tense. Buck truly believes what he's saying about Luke.

I know better, of course. Luke is everything to me. A beautiful and gentle soul. A man who waited for me. He waited until I was ready to make love after what I've been through. A man who feeds stray dogs outside his restaurant.

A man.

A good man.

Buck continues talking. "He's a drug lord. And he uses people. He hurts people, Katelyn. He hurts people."

I don't reply. Not yet. Instead I take a good look at Antonio Moreno. He believes what he's saying. No doubt about that.

"It's still possible that Luke and Lucifer Raven are two different people," I say.

Do I believe my words? I'm not sure. But I do believe one thing—that Luke is a good man. No matter what he did in the past, today—here, now—he's a good man.

"He's lying to you," Buck continues. "Lucifer is not capable of love. He thought he loved my sister, and he mistreated her badly."

"Do you believe a person can change?" I ask.

"I do, actually. I've seen a lot of shit in my life. I've been on missions for the SEALS that would make your blood run cold. And I've seen a man change. Both for the good and for the bad. So yeah, a person can change. But Lucifer? He was just too far gone, sweetheart. Just too fucking far gone."

"You think you know him better than I do?"

"Maybe I don't. But my sister does. They lived together. They were a couple for over a year, and she thought the same thing you do. She thought he was amazing at first. He showered her with luxuries and—"

"Luke hasn't showered me with anything. He's a waiter."

"He's masquerading as a waiter."

"Maybe. Maybe not. But the fact remains that he hasn't showered me with anything. Only his love."

"He turned evidence. Apparently. I'm guessing, of course, because there's no record of where he went. He just disappeared into thin air from his hospital bed after his shoulder healed."

"Do you think he went into the witness protection program?"

"I have sources at the FBI, and there's no record of him."

"Why would they share those records with you? I mean,

isn't that *why* there's a witness protection program? So people like you can't go after those guys?"

"I'm not a criminal, sweetheart. I was just looking for information from valued sources. Sources who knew I was no threat. Believe me, if Lucifer was in the witness protection program, I'd know it."

"Then we must be talking about two different people."

"Two different people with the exact same tattoo?"

I'm grasping at straws, and I know it. "I haven't seen the tattoo you're describing, and you haven't seen the one I'm describing. They could be completely different."

Buck doesn't answer. He just stares at me, refusing to escape my gaze. His brown eyes are burning into me, and I don't like the feeling. I don't like the feeling at all.

With his gaze, he's telling me I'm full of shit. That it's clear Luke and Lucifer are the same person. That I'm an idiot for not believing him.

There's only one straw left, and I grip it between my fingers. "If Luke and Lucifer are one and the same, how did he disappear without the help of the government?"

"He probably got help from his father. Lucifer Ashton Junior is blueblood rich. Old family money."

There goes my last straw.

I sigh. Except it doesn't come out like a sigh. It comes out like a high-pitched squeak as I gulp back a sob.

"It's okay," Buck says. "If you need to cry, cry. I'm used to women's tears. I've listened to my sister cry on more than one occasion. Usually having to do with your boyfriend."

I shake my head. *No. No. No.* Can't be. It's not. He's wrong. He's wrong he's wrong he's wrong.

Except that he's right.

"You're probably wondering why you're here," Buck says.

"No."

"You're not?" He raises his eyebrows.

"If you're right—if Luke and Lucifer are the same person—I think it's pretty clear why I'm here."

"They think that by taking you they can ferret him out. But Lucifer is concerned with only one person, and that's himself."

"You don't think he'll come for me?"

"Sweetheart, I wouldn't bet a penny on it."

I don't know what to say. I feel sick all over, and when a knock sounds on the door, I don't even jump.

My nerves have gone on hiatus. I just don't care anymore. Why? What's the point?

Buck goes to the door and opens it.

He comes back with a tray of food. "I guess it's lunchtime. Or dinnertime. Who the hell knows?"

"Why didn't you run out?"

"Because I'm not a moron."

"You can do something, can't you? You could've punched his face. You're a big guy."

"Sweetheart—"

"*Stop* calling me that," I hiss.

"Sorry. Katelyn, I just told you I'm not a moron. You think the drug kingpin keeping us here doesn't have this place fully surrounded? We wouldn't get five feet before we were shoved back in here, and then we'd be punished for attempting to escape."

"But shouldn't we at least try?"

"Absolutely. And we will. As soon as I figure out a viable way to get us out of here. But we have to think it through. And right now, I don't know the lay of the land."

"Maybe I can help."

"Exactly how can you help? I'm sorry, but you were held on an island for ten years, and you can bet this place has equal security. You didn't get anywhere."

"I could..." The thought that comes into my head is disgusting, but I have to say it. "I could...seduce him."

"Sure. I have no doubt you'd be successful. But first of all, I won't allow you to put yourself in that position, and second of all, while you're seducing one, ten more will come after me."

He's right.

"Then what?" I ask.

"We eat our food to keep up our strength. And we wait."

"For what?"

"For an opportunity to present itself."

"What if they hurt us?"

"They may very well try to hurt me. But you?" He shakes his head. "You, they won't touch. Not until they have to."

Buck's words slice into me like an icy blade.

Not until they have to.

I'm not sure what he means.

But I know none of it is good.

45

LUKE

I spend the next several minutes continuing to investigate the room I'm locked in. Funny how many chances King has given me to escape. Except he knows I won't. It would be a futile attempt.

The window. He gave me a windowed room. A nail file and the razor blade. The pen.

He's banking on me putting myself first.

He doesn't realize I'm not that man anymore. Someone is more important to me than my own life, and I will fight to the death for her. To keep her safe.

All I have so far is a freaking toilet tablet. I don't dare take the one from my toilet in this room, for fear they will check everything.

For now, I wait.

HOURS PASS before someone knocks on the door. I'm shocked that King is allowing me the benefit of a knock.

"Who is it?"

"Supper."

The granola bars still sit on the table beside the bed. I'm not hungry, but I need to eat.

"Come on in." Not like I have a choice.

The door opens. The same guy stands there, the driver. He carries a tray containing a plate covered with a silver dome. "Here you go."

I take the tray from him. "Any good news?" I ask.

"Not that I could tell you."

"What's in this for you, man?"

"I've got a family to feed."

"Do you? Because if you cross these guys, they won't think twice about bringing your family in here to use."

"You think I don't know how it is?"

"I'm pretty sure you *do* know how it is. For example, you know there's a woman in this house. A woman I care for. And the man you work for? He's going to harm her to get to me."

The driver says nothing.

"What's your name, man?"

"Grunt number one."

I scoff. "You think you're number *one*?"

"I was kidding, dude. He doesn't care what my name is. And neither do you."

"That's where you're wrong. I *do* care. I'm not the guy King has told you I am."

"We all know you are, man. And we all know why you're here."

"You think so?"

"Of course. We know why your woman's here too."

"And you're okay with that? With letting an innocent

woman be harmed because of something your boss thinks *I* did?"

"None of my business, dude."

"Isn't it? Look, I've been where you are. I was the driver once. I was grunt number 356 or whatever the fuck you are. I moved up. I moved up quickly."

"Maybe that's what I want."

"Do you? Because I guarantee you it's not. I thought it was what I wanted but turns out it wasn't. It was the worst part of my life."

"And yet...here you are. Back here."

"You're right. I'm back here because he threatened someone I love. I will gladly give my life for hers."

"Here's the thing you need to remember," the guy says. "He doesn't give a rat's ass about her life. She's here to control you. The life he gives the shit about...is yours."

Not such a moron after all. This guy understands the stakes. "You're smarter than I gave you credit for. I apologize."

"No need to. I know what I'm doing. I've got a family to feed. I'm not sure if you know the situation here in LA, but life ain't great."

"There are jobs available."

"There are. But I can't support my family on fifteen bucks an hour. You know the cost of living here. I'm not qualified to do anything more than that."

"Funny that you're talking to me like this." I cast my gaze around the room. "I don't see any surveillance equipment. I'm shocked, to tell you the truth, that he's not recording me. My every move."

"Maybe he is."

"And you'd be speaking so freely if he were?"

"Maybe I'm working from a script. There's a lot you don't know."

This guy is smart. Really smart. No, he's not working from a script. I know King's MO well enough to know that. But damn, this kid is smart.

"Do yourself a favor," I say. "Go get yourself one of those fifteen-dollar-an-hour jobs. You've got a brain in your head, man, and you'll move up the ladder quickly if you do a good job."

"What I'm lacking is patience. I need the money now for my family."

"You're making a mistake."

"I'm not doing anything differently than you did."

"True enough. In fact, your motives are a lot purer than mine were. Hell, I didn't need the money. I just wanted to stick it to my old man. Stick it to my way of life."

"Oh?"

"How much do you know about me?"

"I only know what the boss tells me."

"You and I both know that's not true. You can find out about me from any news source."

He says nothing.

"I'm willing to bet you know everything about me. At least everything that's in the public eye."

No reply.

Finally, he says, "I've got to get back."

"Sure. I get it. Think about this, though. If you can get the woman out of here, I will owe you. I will owe you big."

"I don't think—"

"Before you go any further, listen to me, and listen good. My life isn't worth shit. We both know that. But I have money, man. A trust fund. It's yours. Half of it, anyway. You need to split it with her. It'll take care of your family for years to come."

"How do I know you can even make that happen?"

"I'll give you a message to get to my old man. If he knows you helped me, he'll do as you ask."

"If I try to leave, my life is as worthless as yours."

He's only a little bit wrong. Everyone's life is worth more than mine in this organization right now. But if he crosses King, he'll definitely be on the list.

"Well," I say, "it was worth a shot."

He's not ready. He's not ready to give up his own life. That's where he and I are different. I'm willing to give up my own life for Katelyn's. If he were ready, he'd have jumped at my offer.

He turns to leave, but then he looks over his shoulder. "How much money are we talking?"

"Enough that your family will never have to worry about earning a dime, and neither will any of their progeny."

He turns, stares at the door, and then looks back at me again. "Tell me what I have to do."

46

KATELYN

Buck hands me a plate of food. It's chicken breast and broccoli. Hash browns or something that looks kind of like hash browns. A roll with butter. And a glass of water.

"How do we know it's not poisoned?"

"Because that's not this guy's style. They're not going to hurt you until they have to."

I wince again at those words.

"I'm sorry. I know you don't like to hear me talk like that. I know you've been through hell in your short life. I wish I could make this easier on you."

"Do you? Do you really? If you really wanted to make it easier on me, you'd lie to me. Tell me what I want to hear."

"That wouldn't make it easier on you, sweetheart. Sorry...I mean Katelyn." He picks up a roll and bites into it harshly, as if he's ripping the head off a chicken or something.

He's angry. Even in his eating, he's angry. Why shouldn't he be? He's being held here just as I am. Against his will.

The only difference is he began this quest to find Luke. He has a reason for being here.

I'm here as an innocent bystander.

I pick up my steak knife—yes, they gave us steak knives—and slice off a piece of the chicken. Then I hold up my knife. "Can't you do something with this?"

"First of all, they're not going to let us keep these utensils. They'll be back to collect them as soon as they think they've given us enough time to eat, so eat quickly."

"But still—"

"Katelyn, these people we're dealing with are not stupid. And they know we're not stupid. They know I won't try anything with a steak knife. And even if I did, they'd be well prepared."

I nod. "So we're really on our own?"

"We are. I'll get us out of here, but you need to let me do it on my time. I'll figure a way out. I always do."

I nod. I cut another piece of the chicken, the serrated blade of the steak knife grinding against the ceramic of the plate.

I remember again... The plate I hid under my mattress.

And what I paid for it.

DIAMOND HESITANTLY LEADS *me through the dorm and outside.*

"Where are you taking me?"

"I'm so sorry, Moonstone."

"I don't understand."

"You're going on a hunt," she says.

"In daylight?" It's not unheard of, but most of the hunts take

place at night. It's more of a challenge that way. The guys who come here live for the challenge. In their warped minds, hunting defenseless women at night is a challenge. "Who requested me?"

"No one requested you. This is a special occasion."

"What kind of special occasion?"

"You'll be hunted. Hunted by...all of the men here on the island."

"What?" *Have I heard her correctly?*

Normally only one person is allowed to hunt one of us at a time. And normally I don't get hunted that often. It's only happened a few times before.

More often I get taken by someone who wants to talk to me, sometimes beat me, sometimes rape me.

Then there's Ice Man.

All he does is pee on me. It's humiliating and awful and I hate it, but...at least I live through it.

It's a sunny day on the island. Sometimes it rains, but not today. How can I hide anywhere on the hunting ground when the sky is blue and there's nothing to camouflage me?

"Get in," *Diamond says.*

"Diamond, please..."

She cups my cheeks. "I wish I could change this for you. I wish I could take the punishment instead of you."

She seems sincere. But is she? I never know. She keeps doing what she does, all the while saying how terrible it is. But still...she does it.

She opens the passenger door side of the Jeep.

I don't move.

"Get in," *she says again.* "If you don't, I have to give you this." *She pulls a syringe out of her pocket.* "Please don't make me do that, Moonstone. If I do, you'll be drugged. You won't be able to run as quickly. Believe me. You don't want me to have to do this."

I relent and get into the Jeep.

"You know the drill." She hands me a hood.

Yes, we're hooded when we go to the hunting ground. I never really understood why. I can't think of one of us who would go there on our own if we knew the way.

The ignition roars to life, and the Jeep begins moving. It's a hot tropical day, and the black fabric of the hood absorbs heat, making it difficult for me to breathe.

Or perhaps it's my racing heart. At least I won't hyperventilate with the hood on. I'll be breathing a lot of carbon dioxide.

Despite the heat, goosebumps erupt over my flesh. Diamond didn't give me any special clothes to wear. I'm wearing shorts and a T-shirt, what we girls always wear in the dorm.

This means only one thing.

She will take my clothes when we get to the hunting ground. I'll be naked. Naked and at the mercy of whoever catches me.

Sometimes we're given weapons. Simple things like a fork or a chopstick. Garnet has done some real damage with a chopstick. She's a natural athlete and boy, does she fight.

Which is, unfortunately, one of the reasons she's so popular on the hunt. She gives a good fight. Apparently the men like that. She's worthy prey.

That's what they call her. Worthy prey.

I remember the two men saying that about me before I was brought to the island. They called me worthy prey. I only met one other woman in that concrete dungeon. I told her to go. I told her to kill me, but when she wouldn't, I told her to go. To escape.

Although both my shoulders were dislocated, I eventually forced myself to get up and move.

That's when they decided I was worthy prey.

Despite that fact, I've been to the hunting grounds rarely.

I don't know why that is. Something about the way I look. I'm in decent shape—we all are—but I'm not a natural athlete like Garnet.

"Diamond," I say, my voice muffled through the hood, "I didn't use the plate. Doesn't that count for something?"

She doesn't reply.

I suppose it's easier for her now that she doesn't have to look me in the eye.

Or she supposes that replying would do me no good. She has to do what she has to do, apparently. I've often wondered who she is, and why she does this.

But I've never asked. Some of the other girls have, and she doesn't give any answer. Not surprising.

Every nerve in my body is on alert, as if I'm already out there being hunted.

I clear my throat. "How many men will there be?"

Again, Diamond doesn't respond.

"Please, Diamond. Tell me something. Anything that could help me."

I hear a sigh. Then, "I can't, Moonstone. You and I both know that I can't."

I don't say anything else for the remainder of the trip. All I do is think. I think about my cousins—second cousins, actually—Jared and Tony, whose fault it is that I'm here. I think about the other women—Garnet, Tiger Eye, Onyx, Crystal, and so many others—who have survived worse than I have.

I try to console myself with the fact that they won't kill me.

Except...

Will they?

Now that I was caught with a potential weapon, do they mean to get rid of me?

"Diamond!"

"Yes?"

"Are they going to kill me?"

She doesn't reply at once, but just when I'm sure she's not going to at all—

"I don't know, Moonstone. I just don't know."

47

LUKE

An ember of hope flickers in me.

This guy could totally be playing me. I know that. But I have to try. For Katelyn, I must try.

"Tell me everything you can," I say, "about this place. About what's going on here."

"They're going to wonder why I'm taking so long in here," he says.

"Yeah. You're right. At least give me your name."

"My real name is Felix de Soto. Here I'm known as Cardinal."

For the first time I notice his red hair. "That's an apt nickname. King likes to use bird names."

"What do you need me to do?"

"Find an excuse to get back here. Let me know what's going on."

"I can tell you that your woman is here."

"I already know that."

"You do?"

"I do. I can feel her."

He lifts his eyebrows. "You feel her?"

"Yeah. Can't you feel your wife?"

"I don't know. She's not here, so how could I?"

"But you'd know if she were in trouble."

"Maybe."

"Look. I don't have time to explain this weird psychic thing going on. It's something I've never felt before. But yeah, I know she's here. What else you got?"

"King. King is here."

I nod. I've known that all long as well. I feel him too, in a totally different way than I feel Katelyn's presence. But I don't say it. I don't want to have to defend my psychic bullshit again.

"Your woman is here. There's a guy in with her."

Rage, my old, flawed friend, spears through me once more. "What?" I say through gritted teeth.

"Yeah, some dude we caught casing the perimeter of this place. A big dude."

"And why the hell did they put him in with Katelyn?"

"There was no place else to put him. We weren't expecting him."

My hands curl into fists.

"He hasn't hurt her."

"He damned well better not."

"I think he's a good guy."

"And you, Cardinal. Are you a good guy?"

"If I weren't, do you think I'd be trying to help you?"

I nod. "Good enough. Get back here as soon as you can. I need more information. And if you can sneak anything in here that I can use for a weapon—something they can't foresee—I'll gladly take it."

"I don't think that will help. They frisk me every time I go in and out."

"Got it. I understand."

Then he winks. He's going to do something.

"I'll be back to get your tray in a bit," he says. Then he shuts the door behind him.

I eat my dinner or lunch whatever the hell it is. And wait.

About twenty minutes later, as far as I can tell, Cardinal returns to take the dishes.

He doesn't speak this time. When he leaves, he closes the door very carefully.

The lock does not click.

Eureka.

He's given me a chance. A chance to escape. He didn't do it before because he knew he'd have to come back shortly to get the tray and then report.

This way I have more time. He won't have to report that I'm missing until the next time he comes in.

Already I know guards are perched outside the window. Already I know they're prepared for the pen, the razor blade, the nail file.

I also know that no one is watching the door at this moment. If someone were, they would know it's not shut.

This is my window of opportunity.

I know King. He has many minions stationed here.

I don't bother taking the razor blade, the file, or the pen.

Much better to leave them here, to let them think I'm unarmed. All I have is a toilet tank tablet in my pocket. I'll have to rely on whatever chemicals are in it, which means I'll have to make direct contact with someone's eyes.

The hallway is well lit, and there's another door.

Katelyn could be behind that door. I rush toward it. Key

in the numbers that I've memorized. There's not a huge chance that this the same combination, but I have to try.

No luck.

But then a voice. A man's voice. "Who's there?"

"Do you know the combination?" I ask. "I'll get you out of there.

Whoever is in there may have memorized it, like I did, when Cardinal opened the door.

"Yeah," he says, "it's 7947."

I key in the combination quickly, and the door clicks open.

Katelyn stands in the background, and she lets out a gasp. "Luke!"

"You," the other man says.

His punch comes quickly to my left jaw.

In a flash I'm on the floor.

"No!" Katelyn yells. She runs toward me. "Luke!"

"You fucking son of a bitch."

I move my jaw. It's not broken, but damn it hurts. I know this man. Emily's brother. Buck Moreno. The guy who shot me.

"I'm here to help." I stand. "You can beat the shit out of me if you want, if it makes you feel better. They're going to kill me anyway. But I'd much rather you get her the hell out of here."

"No," Katelyn says. "I'm not going anywhere without you."

"Katelyn, baby, please. Let this guy take care of you. I'm the one they want. The only reason you're here is because of me."

"I don't care. I won't leave you."

"Please. If you love me, do this. Do this for me. I can't..." I shake my head. "They'll hurt you, Katelyn. They'll hurt you

to get to me. You've been hurt enough. I'm so sorry. Please...
Just go."

Buck turns to her. "He's right. I'll try to get us out of here."

"No." She shakes her head, tears glistening in her eyes. "I
can't. I can't lose you, Luke. I just can't."

Time for me to get stern. "That's not my name."

"I don't care what your real name is. You'll always be Luke
to me."

Time for some tough love. Time for her to think that she
needs to leave no matter what. Time to call on my untrustworthy friend.

"Go," I grit out. "I'm not Luke. My name is Lucifer. Lucifer
Raven. I'm the fucking devil, Katelyn. Go."

"I can't."

I turn to Buck. "Get her the fuck out of here. Now."

Buck grabs her hand. "Come on." He drags her out of the
room.

She looks over her shoulder at me.

And I know what I have to do.

"It's over," I say, hating myself for the words. "You and I
aren't going to happen. Ever. Now go."

He drags her up the stairs and through a doorway.

Will they make it out? I don't know, but I pray to a God
I'm not sure exists that they do.

*Take me. Do whatever you want to me. Just let her live. Let her
have a happy life. Please don't hurt her anymore.*

48

KATELYN

My head is throbbing, my body numb.

He didn't mean it. Luke didn't mean it. He *will* come for me. He didn't mean it when he said we were over, that we'll never happen.

I want to sob, but I don't dare. Buck holds his finger to his mouth to signal me to be quiet.

So I gulp back my sobs. I force my body to move. To follow Buck, to keep my hand secured in his.

I don't know where we're going.

At this point, I'm not sure I care.

But I must find that strength that I found that day on that hunt. I must find it and hold onto it, because my life—and Luke's—depends on it now.

∽

"Go."

Diamond removes the hood and then repeats the word.

"Go."

I nod. There's no use in fighting. I know better.

I'm surprised when she doesn't take my clothes. I could ask why, but then she may just be alerted to the fact that I'm still wearing them. Best to keep them as long as I can. I don't need them in this tropical climate, but they at least give me some semblance of modesty. Someone will take them from me soon.

The hunting ground. It's like a tropical rain forest. It takes up a good portion of the island, and it's fenced in. Ten-feet-high pickets with barbed wire. No one can get out except through the gate that I walk through now. It's quiet so far. Insects chirp, and a few birds fly in the air. Tropical birds that are colorful—colorful and happy. Do they have any idea what they fly above? Do they hear the screams of the women in this hunting ground and sing for us?

If only... If only I had wings like a bird so I could fly away. Far away. Of course, I'm not exactly sure where I am. Most likely my wings would give out before I hit another island.

Still...I can dream. I can dream that someday I'll fly out of here.

That day, however, is not today.

My job today is to survive.

I walk through the gate purposefully, not looking over my shoulder to see Diamond in the Jeep. A few seconds later, I hear her throw it into gear and drive away.

I haven't been in the hunting ground as many times as a lot of the others, but still I've learned to keep all my senses on alert. My nose for anything that smells out of place. Fire perhaps, or some kind of chemical product.

My sight. Today of course the sun is out and it's broad daylight. I'll be able to see a lot farther than usual because we normally come here in the dark.

My ears. I keep them perked for sounds. The hunters like to

move quietly, so I've learned to pick up on the smallest crack of a twig under their foot. The shallowest breath.

Even taste. Sometimes, the humidity is so thick I can taste it, and I know that the men will move more slowly.

Unfortunately, the humidity is not as thick today. They'll be able to move quickly. Diamond told me all the men on the island will come. That could be three or thirty. I just don't know.

First things first. I need to find water. I've been here before, so I know where a few streams are. I head toward one of them and drink my fill. Then I hide.

The trees are thickest on the north side. I head there.

Unfortunately, there aren't any caves to hide in. Or perhaps there are and I just never found them. Some of the women talk about their experiences during the hunt. They help each other. But in a way, they're not helping. The more they talk, the more women use their particular tricks, and the more men figure them out.

I've chosen to keep my tricks to myself. Unfortunately, that means if there is a cave or other hiding place like that, I don't know where it is.

I move as quietly as I can in the thicket. Not staying in one space for too long.

Until—

I hear them. The rustling. They're not even trying to hide their steps.

They're coming for me. They're coming for me in droves.

Then the smells. The acrid scent of their body odor. Tobacco, booze. The alcohol that pours out of their pores.

They're always meaner when they're drunk.

This is not a hunt.

This is an ambush.

And I'm frightened for my life.

But damn it, if I'm going to go down, I'm going to go down fighting.

The first body lands on top of me. I kick and scream and scratch and claw, drawing blood on his forearm as he tries to hold me down. I bring my knee up to his crotch and—

"Bitch!"

He tumbles off me and I jump into a stand.

Another one is on me in an instant. I use an old trick I learned from a self-defense lesson back in high school gym. Before he can trap my arms, I grab the sides of his head and push my thumbs through each of his eye sockets, blinding him.

I push him off me and stand again.

"This one knows her stuff," one man says.

Some are masked and some aren't. I don't know how many there are. I can't stop to count. I kick one, punch another. Another takes me down, this time making sure my hands are taken care of so I can't take his eyes.

However, he leaves his privates unguarded, and I give him the knee.

I begin to stand again but before I reach my feet, two more are upon me. I kick, I scratch, I scream and yell, bite the lobe off one of their ears. I'm pounded then. Punched. Cut.

Still I stay strong.

I don't stop fighting. I don't stop... Until blackness envelops me.

I wake up later back in the dorm. Diamond is sitting with me.

"Diamond?" The word comes out as a squeak.

"You're awake. Don't try to talk. Your jaw is slightly cracked. You don't need to have it wired shut, but you do need to take it easy. Let it heal for the next couple weeks.

My jaw is the least of my issues. I hurt everywhere. I especially hurt between my legs. They must have...

They must've had their way with me after I lost consciousness.

"We have a few necrophiliacs in the bunch," Diamond says, as if reading my mind.

I say nothing.

"They used you pretty badly. Do you remember any of it?"

Do I?

I remember fighting. I remember kicking a couple of them in the balls. Pushing one's eyes out.

"Eyes," I squeak out.

"Yes. You did a number on that one. He won't be back here for a while."

"Good," I say.

"You did well out there. As good as Garnet or any of the others could've done. You didn't stop fighting, Moonstone. You found your strength."

Yes. I found my strength. And I will survive here. But I won't survive as Katelyn.

To survive here, I must be Moonstone. No one but Moonstone. Moonstone takes no prisoners.

MOONSTONE. I truly thought I had left her on that island. After that hunt, I threw myself into being Moonstone. I left Katelyn behind, to the point that I didn't even remember my name until Zee came to the island and called me Katelyn.

But Katelyn can't survive this. Even with Buck's help.

No.

I need Moonstone.

Moonstone must come back.

And Moonstone takes no prisoners.

49

LUKE

I have only one job now. To make sure Katelyn and Buck get the hell out of here safely.

I know this place is guarded, but Buck is smart. He was a Navy SEAL, and he's a crack shot. A sniper. He doesn't have a gun on him, but he knows how to move stealthily.

I must depend on him. I have no other choice. The man hates me, and for good reason. But he's a search-and-rescue guy, and if anyone can keep Katelyn safe, Buck can.

My job is to keep them out of harm's way. If that means sacrificing my own life? I will do it without regret.

I follow them. As Buck and Katelyn move quietly, hiding in whatever shadows they can find, I move not so quietly.

If King's going to find anyone, he's going to find me.

I make noise going up the stairs. And I find no guard situated at the top. Good. That means Buck and Katelyn got out.

But also not good.

Something's up.

I walk through the house, and I walk out the door.

No guards that I can see. They could be hidden. But if they were, they would stop me.

Something doesn't make sense here.

And I don't like it. I don't like it one bit—

I crumple to the ground, electric currents slashing through me. Damn! I try to scream out but I can't, my vocal cords don't work. My body shakes, and I have to piss. Really fucking have to piss.

Someone grabs me.

Harsh hands pull me to my feet while I continue to shake.

A few minutes later I gain control of my nerves once again, and I'm being dragged back into the house into a different room. This one has windows.

I try to assess the situation, but my body is still weak from the tase. Now what? How many men are there? My vision is blurred, but one is holding me up, forcing me forward.

Where are the others? I can't tell. They're everywhere, most likely, but I must take this chance. I need to give Buck and Katelyn more time.

I reach into my front pocket, grab the toilet tank tablet encased in toilet paper, and scrunch it hoping like hell I get enough chemical on my fingers to do some damage.

I'm looking at getting tased again, possibly even shot. This doesn't matter. I have to do what I can. I have to give Buck and Katelyn more time to get the hell away from here.

My vision is still blurry, but I press my weight into the body holding me, knocking him off balance.

"For God's sake, you son of a bitch," a voice says. "What are you going to do next? Piss your pants?"

Piss my pants? And it dawns on me. He thinks I'm reacting to the taser.

Good. That's good.

I say nothing, but I wait a few seconds, and then I push against him again, this time overpowering him and bringing us both to the ground. I'm on top of him, and I bring my hand to his face and press my fingers against one of his eyes.

"Shit!" He squeezes his eyes shut.

I quickly rub my fingers against the other one. And then I rise, my body still like jelly.

I grab his gun. Then I grab the taser as well. I don't want to harm anyone, and the taser will help me with that. But I need the gun.

I don't know how long this guy will be indisposed. He's writhing on the ground, rubbing his eyes, wailing. I quickly stuff my hand in one of his pockets. Nothing. Then another. Bingo. I find a cell phone and grab it.

This way King won't be able to communicate with him.

Now what? I don't have anything to tie him up with—no rope or duct tape. I shove my hand back in my pocket, ready to give him more chemical in his eyes, but then I think better of it. I don't know who else I'm going to have to overpower, so I need to save whatever chemicals I have. I could tase him, but that won't last long. I could shoot him, but I don't want to. I don't want to harm anyone if I don't have to.

I've done enough of that in my life.

I'm going to go out without killing anyone, if possible.

My own eye itches, but I don't dare scratch it. My fingers are still full of chemicals, and I need my vision. It's still not completely back from the tase, so I can't compromise it.

"Where is he?" I ask the guy. "Where's King?"

He doesn't answer. He's still screaming and wailing, and his eyes are shut, tears squeezing out of them.

"Answer me, asshole." I stick the nose of the gun on his forehead.

"Please, please don't."

"Tell me."

"You're going to fucking blind me. Get me some water for my eyes."

"You're not in a position to be making demands. Now tell me. Where the fuck is King?"

"I... I don't know. Upstairs I think."

"And the others? The man and the woman? Did they get away?"

"What man and what woman?"

Good. He could be lying, but maybe he isn't. Maybe Katelyn and Buck got away.

"I'm out of here," I say.

"No! Wait! My eyes!"

I don't respond. With the gun in my right hand, the taser in my left, I trudge back to the house.

I enter, find the stairs, and ascend as quietly as I can. I stop at the top of the landing and lean against the wall. I inhale deeply. *Get with it, Luke. You can do this. Get control of your fucking body.*

I open my eyes. Exhale.

Time's up.

50

KATELYN

We're ambushed before we leave the yard.

Damn it. Buck throws his body in front of mine. "Stay behind me," he whispers.

"I can hold my own," I tell him.

"They probably have guns, Katelyn. Are you bulletproof?"

"Are you?"

He says nothing.

A man grabs my wrists and duct tapes them together.

I lean closer to him lift my knee and—

He screams out as I kick him in the nuts.

Buck takes over then. He smashes my guy on the head and then executes some kind of kick to the other guy who was attempting to duct tape Buck's wrists.

His wrists are still free. He grabs me and yells, "Run!"

I run.

I run.

I have no idea where I'm going, no idea if Buck is behind me. But I run. I'm Moonstone, and I run.

Until—

I cry out as someone tackles me to the ground.

"No!" I use all my strength to try to pry my wrists apart, but I cannot free myself.

"I ought to give you a lesson right here, bitch." The voice comes from above me.

"Don't you touch her!" Buck's voice.

I'm on the ground, face down. My bound wrists underneath me, my shoulders aching.

They're not dislocated again, but they're in a really awkward position because of my bound wrists.

Swat!

Something comes down on my ass.

"That's for running."

Anger wells up in me. I am Moonstone, and I will fight. Using all my strength, I roll onto my back.

A man stands above me, and I quickly weave my feet around his ankles and bring him to the ground.

"Bitch!" He stands up and pulls me up by my bound wrists. "You'll pay for that, whore."

But he doesn't scare me. I've taken more than this man even knows about.

Buck is standing a few feet away, his wrists now bound like mine. Another man has a gun to his back.

I hold back a gasp.

We could lose our lives here. That was one thing I didn't have to worry about on the island. They could take me to the brink of death, but they couldn't kill me.

These men? They aren't bound by those directives.

I'm not ready to die. I'm not ready to give up on Luke, no matter what he did.

I am Moonstone. Moonstone was forged in battle, and I will fight.

"You do as I say, you dumb bitch, or I'm going to shoot your friend here in the back."

Buck's expression is noncommittal. How can he be so calm? Military training, I suppose. He's always been ready to give his life. It's what Navy SEALs do.

"Who let you out?" the man holding me asks.

I work up a loogie and spit in his face.

Smack! The palm of his hand stings my cheek.

"Don't you lay a hand on her again," Buck says through gritted teeth.

"You shut up, you motherfucker, or I'll end your life right here," the guy holding the gun on him says.

My cheek tingles from the smack, but it doesn't hurt. I've been beaten way worse than this. This is no more than a scratch.

"I asked you a question," the guy on me says. "Who let you out?"

I say nothing.

Smack! And then another.

"You answer me, damn it. Or I will kill you."

I have no doubt that he will. But I will not give Luke up.

Buck apparently doesn't have those qualms, though. "It was the Raven. Lucifer Raven."

"Buck, no!" I shout.

"It's him or you," Buck says. "He told me to save you."

Did he? Yes, he did. But then he told me that we were over.

He was lying. He wanted me to get out safely.

I knew that. I've always known that. His words hurt, but they were for my own good.

The only problem is...I'm not sure I want to live without him. Luke showed me there was beauty left in the world.

I need him.

And he needs me.

"Take me to him," I say.

"You're giving me orders now?" the guy holding me says.

"Take me to Luke. I mean Lucifer."

"For the love of God, Katelyn, shut the fuck up," Buck says.

I shake my head. "If Luke is going down, so am I."

"That's not what he wants." Buck again.

"Both of you shut the fuck up," the guy holding a gun on Buck says.

The two men push us back toward the house.

No.

This isn't happening. I'm not giving up this easily.

Moonstone. I'm Moonstone. In a flash, I'm back on the island. Back on the island where I'm determined to fight.

I turn quickly, raise my arms, my wrists still bound, knee the man in the balls while at the same time I bring my two fists to the side of his head.

He falls to the ground, bringing his knees up to his chest. "Fucking whore!"

That spurs Buck into action. Despite the gun in the middle of his back, he turns and executes an amazing kick to the side of the guy's face. Then he grabs his gun.

"Run!" he shouts at me.

I turn and run, my wrists still bound. Is he following me? I don't know. I have to believe he is.

But the problem is, as I run, I'm getting farther and farther away from Luke. I stop, turn around.

"Damn it, I said run!" Buck yells.

"No. I'm not leaving him."

"He wants you safe!"

"But he means everything to me. I don't expect you to understand." My heart is beating so fast. "I have to do this."

"Then you're on your own."

"So be it." I begin walking back toward the house.

"Wait!"

"What?"

He hands me the gun. "Take this."

I take the gun from his hands, its casing hot against the palm of my bound hand. "I don't know how to shoot. I'm not sure I can with my wrists bound like this."

"Doesn't matter. Just act like you can."

"Is it loaded?"

"It appears to be."

It slips from my hands and lands with a thud onto the grass.

"Damn it. You need to be more careful."

I bend down, pick up the gun. Again it's hot against the palms of my hands.

Buck is right. This will help me. Unless someone gets it away from me and uses it against me.

But that won't happen. Because whoever comes after me will have his own gun.

I'm frightened. More frightened than I've ever been, even that one day on the hunt.

But I suck in a breath. And I think about Luke.

Luke, who's in there, and who needs me.

51

LUKE

I slowly open the door.

King sits behind a desk. "Sit down, Raven."

I hold the gun up. "Not happening."

"Oh, I think it is. Sit."

"And if I don't? You think you can kill me? I'm holding a nine-millimeter and a taser. What the hell do you have?"

"Katelyn."

His voice is icy. No emotion. I'm not sure he's capable of emotion.

"Nice try. Katelyn got away."

"Did she now?"

My heart sinks.

He's probably lying, but I can't take that chance.

So I play the only cards I have. I walk toward his desk, set down the gun and the taser. "Let her go, King. Let her go when you can do whatever you want to me."

"I'm going to do that anyway, Raven. But I think it might make it a little more fun if your lady friend watches."

"No. Not part of the deal."

"And you think you can make a deal?"

I eye the gun and the taser on his desk. Within a millisecond, I can have one in my hand and on his head. I could kill him right now.

But then I go down for murder.

And I wouldn't see Katelyn anyway.

No. This only ends one way. With Katelyn going free, and me in the ground.

"I never suspected it of you, Raven. I never thought you would turn on me."

I say nothing.

"It was the women. The women and the booze. If it weren't for that woman and the booze, you would've never been on that island. You would've never gotten caught."

He's not wrong. Getting caught on that island, getting shot in the shoulder by Buck, was the best thing that ever happened to me.

It led me to Katelyn.

And Katelyn taught me how to love. Not the obsessive emotion that I thought was love, but *real* love. She showed me there were good people in the world. People who would do anything for another.

So that's what I'll do now.

"I'll work with you again," I say. "I'll be your right-hand man, and you never have to worry about me turning. If you just let her go."

"You must think I was born yesterday, Raven."

"Hell no, I don't think you were born yesterday. But my word is good."

"You're forgetting that you gave me your word once before. Then you reneged on it the first time you had a chance."

"I did. I was facing life in prison. What would you have done?"

"I've turned on everyone," he says, "but we're not talking about me."

"You turned tail and ran to Mexico."

"I did. Or at least I made people think I did."

"Then you of all people ought to understand what I did."

"Did I say I didn't understand? I'm in this for myself as much as you are. Your only problem is that I have a hell of a lot more power than you do."

He's not wrong.

But I have something he doesn't. Someone worth dying for.

Two men enter the room then, force me down on a chair. Duct tape my arms to the arms of the chair and my feet to its legs.

King comes toward me then, brandishing what looks like a Swiss Army knife. "We're going to see just how strong you are for this woman, Raven." He walks toward me, cuts my shirt off me deftly with his knife.

And he finds my brand-new tattoo.

"Nice. Even had yourself branded with her name. I guess I never thought you had it in you."

"What? To love someone?"

"Yeah. What happened to the Lucifer Raven who was cold as ice? Whose only idea of love was control and obsession?"

"Anyone can change," I say. "I'm proof of that."

"I heard you got off the sauce."

"I did."

"That's a shame. Nothing to dull your pain."

I inhale, let the breath out slowly. "I can take anything you dish out. Anything. I ask only that Katelyn stay safe."

"We'll see how much you can take." King curls his lips into his trademark serpentine smile.

I don't react. Just meet his gaze, stare him down. Show him my strength. The strength of my love for Katelyn. Harness my old and untrustworthy friend.

Nothing happens for the next few moments.

Finally, I say, "Get with it, will you?"

"We're waiting for a special guest."

My heart falls.

And then the door opens, and I don't have to turn my head over my shoulder to know who it is.

"Katelyn," I murmur.

She didn't get away.

52

KATELYN

"Luke!"

He doesn't turn his head, but I know it's him. His arms and legs are taped to a chair. The two goons holding me throw me into the chair next to him.

I wait for them to tie me or duct-tape me, but they don't.

Before I have the chance to wonder why, the other man in the room—large and menacing—smiles at me.

"I can see why you're so taken with her, Raven."

"Let her go," Luke says, his jaw clenched.

"I don't think I will," the man says.

"It's okay, Luke," I say, trying to sound a lot calmer than I feel.

I want him to know. Want him to know that I want to be here with him more than I want to be anywhere else in the world.

That if I have to leave this life, I want to leave it with him.

"She has nothing to do with what you think I did to you. She's been through hell, damn it, please. Let her go, King."

King? The guy's name is King?

Two guns sit on the desk. My wrists are no longer bound, though my skin is raw where the duct tape was. I'm bruised and battered, and of course they took the gun Buck gave me, but I will fight. I will fight for Luke.

I could grab a gun from the desk.

But the man. The man has a knife.

He nods to the two guys who brought me in. "Leave us," he says. "And lock the door."

"Don't do anything, Katelyn," Luke says. "Please."

"Luke, I—"

"*Please.*"

I can't make that promise. I learned survival on that island, and I will fight to the death if I must.

I will fight for Luke even if he no longer wants to fight for himself.

"Take a look at this," the man says. He points to Luke's shoulder.

The tattoo. The image he sent me over the phone. His new tattoo that says Katelyn.

"It's new," the man says. "It probably still hurts. In fact, he still has his clear bandage on it." He pries his fingers under what looks like plastic wrap and rips it from Luke's shoulder.

Luke winces, but he says nothing.

King holds up some kind of knife. All I see is the sharp steel blade. It sparkles, as the rays of the sun flow through the window and cast their glow on it.

"This man loves you," King says to me. "He's willing to give his life for you. But let's just see how willing he is to suffer for you."

"No, please—"

"Shut up!" King says. "The more you beg for him, the harder I will hurt him."

I clamp my lips shut.

I'm no stranger to knives. I saw the wounds Zee had before I went to the island. They cut the tops of her breasts, and she still bears the scars. She was bleeding when she found me, my shoulders dislocated. I was cut on the island many times.

King moves behind the chair Luke is bound to, places the sharp blade of the knife against his skin.

"You will watch," he says to me. "If you take your eyes from the knife in my hand at any time, I will end his life. If you speak at any time, I will end his life. Is that clear?"

I swallow the lump in my throat. Then I nod.

"This man professes to love you. So much that he got your name tattooed on his skin. What the hell does that mean, anyway? Men do that all the time, get some woman's name tattooed on their skin. Then there's a bad breakup, and before you know it you're Johnny Depp with the word wino tattooed on your body. Do you think this man loves you? That this tattoo is some kind of proof? Let me be the one to burst your bubble. This man—Lucifer Raven—is not capable of loving another human being."

I open my mouth to refute his words, but then I remember.

I cannot speak, or he will kill Luke.

"We'll see how much he loves you." King positions the knife at the top of the K in Katelyn. "How lucky that he chose script. I can make one long cut."

He slices into Luke's flesh.

Luke winces but does not cry out.

I have no choice but to watch as King slices Luke open in the form of the K. It's a shallow cut as far as I can tell, but beads of blood emerge on Luke's flesh.

But Luke's flesh is not paper, and King isn't able to make one swift cut. He has to stop, and then he begins again with the A.

Luke grimaces. Squeezes his eyes shut. But does not let out a sound.

Rage boils inside me. I feel every cut of that knife on Luke's skin as if it were my own.

In fact, I'd rather he be cutting me.

I've been cut before. I can take it.

I force my gaze to stay on King, on the knife marring Luke's beautiful flesh.

He doesn't move, doesn't let out a sound.

Finally, after what seems like an hour of painstaking work, King is finished. Luke now has my name written in his own blood on his shoulder.

"There," King says. "That's much better. Don't you think?" He nods to me.

I keep my mouth sewn shut.

"Answer me."

"You said if I spoke, you would hurt him more. So I won't be speaking."

"So I did." He slices a long cut into Luke's upper arm.

Luke sucks in a breath.

"Since you spoke, he will suffer."

Rookie mistake. I shouldn't have said anything. I won't trip up again. I try to meet Luke's gaze, try to tell him I'm sorry with my eyes.

But he looks straight ahead.

He will not turn and look at me.

"Your boyfriend here has nerves of steel," King says. "But I'm willing to bet he'll crash if I sink this sharp blade into your pretty flesh."

I suck back a gasp. Again, this isn't anything I haven't been through before. However, there is no failsafe. There's nothing stopping this man from killing me.

"You know?" King says. "You have nerves of steel yourself, don't you? Most women would be throwing up at the sight of all this blood."

Does he not know who I am? What I've been through?

What he's doing to Luke is killing me, but I'm no stranger to blood. I'm no stranger to torture of any kind.

Luke still stares straight ahead. He's focusing on something, but I can't tell what.

Then I see how rigid his forearms are. He's working the duct tape. On his right arm.

He's stretching it, and he should eventually be able to slide his arm off of the chair's arm.

That gives me a job to do.

I must keep King busy so he doesn't notice what Luke is doing.

What can I do? If I speak, he'll hurt Luke more.

But maybe...

Maybe I *need* him to hurt Luke. That's the one thing that will hold his attention rapt.

"Stop it!" I cry out. "I can't take it anymore!"

I rise from my chair.

King turns on me, grabs my shoulders throws me back down on the chair.

Good. He's not focusing on Luke right now.

That's what I want.

"I warned you, little lady." He grabs his knife.

He turns and slices it down Luke's other arm. Blood trickles over the raven's beak, his fiery wings.

I wince at the pain it's causing him, but it's working. In my peripheral vision, I see Luke has almost worked his right arm free.

Good.

I rise again.

"Dammit, bitch, I've had enough of your insolence." This time he smacks me on my cheek.

It stings, but I don't care. I'm giving Luke a chance to—

I gasp as Luke plunges the chair forward toward the desk and grabs the gun. Somehow he turns back to us and shoots King in his left ankle.

"Bitch!" King falls to the floor and grabs his left foot.

"Katelyn," Luke yells, holding the gun on King as best he can with his legs still taped to the chair. "The duct tape! The other side of the desk."

I rush around the desk. Duct tape. I don't see—

Then it's there, right in front of me. I hold it up.

"Get him taped up if you can. Can you handle him?

"He's shot."

"I know. But can you handle him? He's big. He's strong."

"He's shot." I kick King's bad leg, and he curls into a fetal position.

"Nice job. First tape his wrists. Then his mouth. His ankles last since he can't get up anyway.

I nod.

"When you're done, get this tape off me."

I work as quickly as I can. I have trouble ripping the duct tape, but I use my teeth and do my best. King squirms, and I move quickly to stay out of his reach. His arms are long and strong, and he can still hurt me until his wrists are bound. He grabs me by the hair, but I turn and bite hard into the flesh of his forearm.

Blood.

I spit out the vile taste of King's blood.

How am I supposed to—

"His nuts. Knee his nuts," Luke yells.

A swift kick between his legs.

And he's immobile for a few moments. I work quickly on his wrists, and then I tape his mouth.

The horrible screaming and cursing stops. Now it's just mumbling.

He's flailing about with his legs, blood spurting out of his injured ankle.

"Get the tape over his wound." Luke says. "We don't want him to bleed to death."

"We don't?"

"No. I'm not going to be responsible for any deaths today."

My Luke. I wasn't wrong about him. He *is* a good man.

Although I wouldn't mind seeing this asshole bleed to death.

"Why hasn't anyone come?" I ask Luke.

"King told them to lock us in. No one will come. This is King's fight. It's personal between him and me."

I rip the tape off Luke's other arm. As he rubs his chafed wrist, I go to work on his legs. Soon he's free, and he stands. He heads straight for the door. "Damn, it's locked."

"Can only be opened from the outside?"

"For anyone else, yes. But King knows how to get out of here."

Luke trudges toward King and rips the duct tape off his mouth. "Tell us how to get out of here, and I'll let you live."

"You just said no one's going to die here today."

"I did say that." Luke scratches side of his head. "Let me put it this way, then. Tell us how to get out of here, and I'll leave you the use of your legs."

"You won't get away with this, Raven."

"I think I already did. Now tell us how to get the fuck out of here."

"I've got men surrounding this building."

"And as soon as I tell them you're out of commission, who do you think they'll listen to?

"We've got two guns too," I say.

"Dumb bitch," King says. "The other one's a taser."

"Then we have a gun and a taser," I say.

Luke, his chest shiny with perspiration and smeared with drying blood from his cuts, kicks King in the gut. "Call her a bitch one more time, and I'm going to leave you a goddamned vegetable. Now"—he aims the gun between King's legs—"tell me how to get out of here, or say goodbye to your *cojones*."

53

LUKE

I cock the pistol.

"Okay, okay," King rasps out. "I—"

The door crashes open.

It's him. Buck Moreno. Emily's brother.

"Buck!" Katelyn screams.

I'm still holding the gun on King's groin.

"We're good," Buck says. "The cops are here. You're safe."

I don't move. I don't lower the weapon.

"Luke," Katelyn cries. "Did you hear him? Everything will be okay now."

The words. It's like I'm underwater. My head is drowning, and only my friend—my untrustworthy friend—can save me.

Rage is all around me, whooshing through my veins like a microscopic worm.

I have King. I can end this now.

Luke, you said no one will lose a life today.

Katelyn. Katelyn's sweet angelic voice.

Then her touch. Her soft and gentle hands on mine.

Give me the gun, Luke. Please.

Let me try. A male voice. Buck.

No! I will. I love him. He needs me.

Katelyn's caress, so sweet and warm.

It's over. It's over, my love.

My love. My only love.

I turn, look into her understanding eyes.

She takes the gun and hands it to Buck.

"You need a doctor," Katelyn says. "You're bleeding."

"I'm fine." But I wince.

All this time, I forced my body not to feel anything. I had to be strong. To protect Katelyn.

But yeah, I could probably use a doctor.

In the distance, sirens blare.

"Everything's okay now, Luke," Katelyn murmurs in my ear. "I love you, and everything's okay."

"I love you too." I kiss her forehead. "So damned much."

SEVERAL DAYS LATER, after hours and hours of questioning, Katelyn, Buck, and I are free to go.

King is finally in custody and his dirty money has been seized.

As for me, my immunity deal still stands. I'm not sure how my old man did it, but I'm a free man.

No more hiding.

I can be Lucifer Ashton again. Except I don't want to be. I only want to be Luke Johnson.

I still have red on my ledger. I always will. I have to live with that. I think about calling Buck, asking him to meet, but Katelyn tells me not to. That the wounds are still too fresh.

So I'm surprised as hell when he calls me.

I meet him for a burger on the beach.

"We'll never be friends," he says.

"Interesting way to say hello."

"I mean it. This isn't a friendly meeting."

"I never imagined it was." I take a bite of burger and wash it down with bottled water.

"I just want you to know that Emily's good. She's happy."

"I'm glad to hear that."

"Are you?"

"I am." I wipe my mouth with my napkin. "Look. I never expect you to forgive me. I never expect her to forgive me. I was fucked up. I'm the first to admit that. But she has nothing to fear from me, and neither do you."

"You can bet I don't."

I resist rolling my eyes. Such a fucking tough guy.

"So what's this for, then? Why are we here?" I ask.

He swallows his bite of burger, takes a drink of his beer. "We're square. You and I. Square."

I nod. "Good. I'm totally good with that."

"Take care of her. Of Katelyn."

"I will. You take care of Emily."

He nods. "Done."

"And..." I stop.

"What?"

"If you ever need anything. Anything at all, I'm here. Just ask. For what you did for Katelyn. I owe you."

He cocks his head slightly. For a moment, I'm not sure he's going to speak again. Until—

"Thanks."

LATER, after Katelyn and I have dinner, we take a moonlit stroll on the beach. Jed pants at our heals.

Her hand is warm in mine, and we're barefoot, the sand tickling our toes. In my pocket is a velvet box containing a diamond ring.

I'm going to propose. I stop, turn, and—

Katelyn's phone buzzes.

"Ignore it," I say.

"I wish, but it could be about my dad."

James's biopsy results were compromised, so the doctors had to take another. Katelyn and her mom have been waiting to hear.

She glances at her phone. Then she gasps.

"What is it?" I caress her cheek, my heart breaking at the terror in her eyes.

"It's my friend Aspen. Garnet from the island. She's missing!"

READ MORE about Luke and Katelyn in *Garnet*, coming May 31, 2022!

Begin the adventure with *Rebel*, available now!

EXCERPT FROM REBEL

Lacey Ward was fucking hot.

Oh, she tried to hide it in her navy-blue blazer and tight-ass high-necked blouse, her dark blond hair pulled into a high ponytail so tight that her facial muscles could barely move, and her unglossed lips pressed into a straight line, but I knew the type.

A fucking tomcat in the sack.

I could tell by her eyes. They were big, blue, and vibrant, and they looked me over as if I were a hunk of USDA prime beef tenderloin.

Yup, a tomcat.

Not that I'd ever know. Hell, not that I cared.

I was here for one reason only—so my mother and siblings could hear the contents of the shithead's will. I already knew he'd left me a fat lot of nothing.

And I didn't care one fucking bit.

Lacey Ward's voice had a rasp to it. A sexy rasp. It wouldn't be a hardship to listen to her for the next few hours. Hell, I didn't even need to listen to the words. I knew what they'd be anyway.

Rock gets nothing.

Fine with me.

"Section Five, distribution of personal property," Lacey said. "All of my mother's jewelry in my possession and in the safe deposit box at First National Bank is hereby bequeathed to my daughter Riley Doris Wolfe."

No surprise there.

"My automobiles, except for the Tesla and the Porsche, are bequeathed to my sons, Roy and Reid Wolfe, with Roy, as the older, to have the first choice. They will then choose alternately. The Porsche is bequeathed to my daughter, Riley Wolfe."

His cars. Daddy's pride and joy. He loved those damned cars more than he ever loved any person in his life, least of all me.

I stopped listening. I sat back, closed my eyes, and basked in the rhythm of Lacey's sexy voice.

Yeah, Rock. Fuck me good, baby. Pound that hard cock into me...

My groin tightened. Hell, I didn't care. Just get this day over with.

That's it, baby. Fuck me. Make me come...

Damn, she'd look good on the back of my bike, that blond hair flowing out of a helmet. Yup, I was a helmet man. No point in splattering my brains all over the place. Now that I had a life I enjoyed, I wanted to keep it that way.

I hated Manhattan. I wanted to go back to Montana, where the sky was big and blue and everything was open. New York was so closed in. And it smelled. Even in this posh Manhattan office, the stench of the streets still wafted in the air.

I looked around. My brother Roy was looking down at his lap, while Reid was ogling Lacey. Not that I blamed him. He'd probably fucked her already.

A spear of jealousy hit my gut. Why? I didn't know. So what if he'd fucked her? Reid fucked anything in a skirt.

My little sister, Riley, sat next to my mother.

Riley... The sight of her brought it all back. We weren't close, and I was sorry about that. I'd been protecting her that day, but she didn't know that, and I could never tell her.

Then of course...Mommie Dearest.

Constance Wolfe.

Bitch extraordinaire, who'd had no issue with turning a blind eye to her husband's extracurricular activities.

My gaze floated back to Lacey Ward. I closed my eyes again and sighed. This was going to be a long day.

"Section Seven, real property…"

Can I please doze off now? The villa in Tuscany, the ski chateau in Aspen, the loft in Paris. Who needed all that shit? I had my small cabin in Montana, a Harley, and a job doing construction. It kept me fit and paid well, enough to pay my mortgage, keep food in my belly, and gas in my bike. I got to spend a lot of time outdoors. Who needed anything else?

Man, that voice…

Sink that big cock into me, Rock. Yeah, just like that…

Then…

Silence.

My eyes shot open.

Five gazes, belonging to my mother, my siblings, and my father's current slut, were darting arrows straight toward me.

A NOTE FROM HELEN

Dear Reader,

Thank you for reading *Raven*. If you want to find out about my current backlist and future releases, please visit my website, like my Facebook page, and join my mailing list. If you're a fan, please join my Facebook street team (Hardt & Soul) to help spread the word about my books. I regularly do awesome giveaways for my street team members.

If you enjoyed the story, please take the time to leave a review. I welcome all feedback.

I wish you all the best!

Helen

Sign up for my newsletter here:

http://www.helenhardt.com/signup

ACKNOWLEDGMENTS

Thank you so much to the following individuals who helped make *Moonstone* shine: Karen Aguilera, Linda Pantlin Dunn, Serena Drummond, Christie Hartman, Kim Killion, and Angela Tyler.